SHEREE FITCH

GRAVESAVERS

A NOVEL

Doubleday Canada

Doubleday Canada and colophon are trademarks.

LIBRARY AND ARCHIVES CANADA CATALOGUING IN PUBLICATION

Fitch, Sheree

The gravesavers / Sheree Fitch.

For ages 10-12.
ISBN 0-385-66073-1

I. Title.

PS8561.I86G73 2005   jC813'.54   C2004-906936-5

Cover image: Clarissa Leahy/Getty Images
Cover and text design: CS Richardson
Printed and bound in Canada

Published in Canada by
Doubleday Canada, a division of
Random House of Canada Limited

Visit Random House of Canada Limited's website:
www.randomhouse.ca

TRANS 10 9 8 7 6 5 4 3

FOR MY FATHER

"You look at the sky, and you wonder what's up there, except what we see, the sun and the moon and the stars. Anything else? Who knows? Not me! Most of the time, I'm just going from minute to minute; I'm trying to get from here to there— all the chores my folks give me, and my own hassles I've got to get through. It's when something unexpected happens that I stop myself and I ask what's going on: what's it all about?"

"Do you find any answers then?"

"No, not really. Only more questions."

—Eric, aged 12, in an interview with Robert Coles
from *The Spiritual Life of Children*

Row row row your boat
Gently down the stream
Merrily, merrily, merrily, merrily,
Life is but a dream.

THE GRAVESAVERS

TODAY

My father says I know how to make a short story long. My mother says I was born with the gift of the gab.

Today, I've got five minutes to speak—if I can. My tongue's all puckered up, like I just bit into a chokecherry, and my fists are clamped tighter than oyster shells. Minnows are swimming in my belly. As for my heart? It's doing a tap-dance routine, beating faster than before the start of any race I've ever run. Ordinarily, I calm myself down by reciting the names of clouds or constellations or all the capitals in every province and territory of Canada.

Today, that's not working.

There must be at least three hundred of us huddled around this gravesite.

What I want to say in my speech is: everything. I've got this hankering, as Harv would say, a notion to tell the whole story. I want to tell John Hindley's story. He can't tell it himself because he's dead. Kaput. History. Long gone—in a manner of speaking.

But *the truth whole truth and nothing but the truth cross my heart hope to die stick a needle in my eye* is a slippery thing. That's why, after I'm introduced, I'll be telling all these good folks a big fat whopping lie. For their own protection.

If I can make it up those steps to the podium without tripping over my own two feet, I'll do my five-minute spiel. Croak it out if I have to. But I'll always know one thing for certain. It's only one part of a story inside of many stories all twisted around each other like a tangled-up mizzenmast. If, like me, your nautical knowledge is almost zero, a mizzenmast is part of a ship. Picture a humongous rope ladder. It can save your life. John Hindley taught me that. How he managed that is the kind of secret that can only be whispered to the clouds: *Cirrus. Cumulus. Nimbus. Stratus. Cirrocumulus. Altostratus.*

YESTERDAYS

— PROPER INTRODUCTIONS —

Next month, I'll be fourteen and I don't believe in ghosts. Nuh-uh. At least, I don't believe in the kind of ghost that can jump out of a mirror and chase you out of a house or anything. But spirits? That's a whole other story.

"The spirit of a person never dies as long as there's someone around to remember them. And you never know who that someone might be," says my grandmother.

It could even be someone as ordinary as me, Cinnamon Elizabeth Hotchkiss. Mostly I go by Minn, but yes, that's Cinnamon like the spice except with a capital C and that's Hotchkiss, not hopscotch or hog-kiss in case you're even halfway thinking of making a joke. The name Cinnamon comes from the buns my mother ate waiting for me to arrive. Also, the song. The one my father sang to her belly in his best country-and-western twang:

O sweet little cinnamon baby
O baby we love you so
Sugar and spice and everything nice
Our sweet little baby-yoooo!

He yodels on the *o*. I know this song well because he still sings it to me. In front of my friends. Get the picture? Raymond—*but hey, you can call me Ray*—Hotchkiss is a real joker, all right. I think he really wishes he could yodel for a living. He's a wannabe Wilf Carter—a famous singer "born right here in Nova Scotia," he loves to boast. He seems to forget we live in New Brunswick and Wilf Carter is long dead. My father gets up every day, yodels in the shower like Wilf and dresses like a Canadian postcard. He's a corporal in the RCMP. That stands for Royal Canadian Mounted Police, by the way, not Rotten Carrots Mashed Potatoes or Really Crazy Mental People. You might not know that if you aren't Canadian.

Being a Mountie's daughter means I get to spit every year on November the tenth. That's when my father polishes his boots for the Remembrance Day parade.

I spit. Corporal Ray polishes. By the time we're through, there I am, staring at my own reflection in the toe of each boot.

"Shinier than any mirror in the whole of Buckingham Palace," boasts Corporal Ray.

But the best part? If I watch real close, I'll catch his wink when he passes by next day in the parade. He's supposed to be at attention and keep his eyes straight ahead like some kind of workhorse wearing blinders. Still, he always manages that wink.

Being a cop's kid isn't all about having fun spitting. It's not all parades.

When I was in Grade Two, Davey Stevenson told me my father was a p-i-g PIG!

"Pig child eat dirt!" he said. I ran home crying and told my mother who told my father.

"Going to tell ya something, Minn," he said that night after supper. "Next time Davey Stevenson tells you I'm a pig you look him right in the eye and say, that's right, Davey, all cops are pigs. P-I-G-S. Stands for Pride, Integrity, Guts and Stamina."

That's exactly what I did next time Davey started in. Shut him up pretty fast, all right.

One night just last year Corporal Ray didn't come home his usual time. When he got home my mother cried and hung on to him for dear life. They tried to spare me the details of what happened. Next day I found out anyhow, in the news. My father was the one who went in to get the bad guy. Buddy had a gun, too, and was holding his family hostage.

I still have nightmares about that one.

When I was little, Corporal Ray used to pretend he

was a horse and cantered all us kids in the neighbourhood around the backyard. One at a time, he'd hoist us
up on his shoulders, then gallop and whinny at the top
of his lungs like some kind of idiot. Being a Mountie's
daughter means you know that the bad guys aren't just
on TV. You know that good guys are real, too.

My mother, Dory, is a consultant for a paint store in
downtown Fairvale. "It's a dream job," she says, "the world
is my crayon book." Office buildings and kitchen cabi-
nets are, too. She mixes the paint, and best of all, she
gets to invent new names all the time. Sombrero Sun.
Cattail Brown. Foxy Cyan. Gumball Blue. That last one
was one of my suggestions, by the way. Her favourite television show is *Paint It Great* and her most prized
possession is an autographed copy of the book written
by the show's host. My mother also loves gardening and
music by the old British singing group the Ladybugs.

"Contrary to popular belief," she says, "not all
Maritimers grew up listening to fiddles and bagpipes."

She's nuts about Hardly Whynot, the lead singer.
"Hardly, sing to me," she says when she puts on a CD.
Then she gets a goopy look in her eyes like he's singing
just for her. Leastways, she used to.

And I used to be the only child of Dory and
Raymond Hotchkiss of 22 Redwood Drive, Fairvale,
New Brunswick. E3B 1Z4. Eat three bananas, one
Zamboni four.

Everything's changed. I'm still the only child. But my folks—as I knew them—vanished for a while. In their place? Two people—Dory and Ray look-alikes. Not Dory and Ray the parents I used to know.

It wasn't their fault. The winter before last, during the week between Christmas and New Year's, a baby died before it was born. Corporal Ray and Dory's baby. Because of what happened that week, and what happened after that and what happened after that, I got to meet John Hindley the way I did.

— THE START OF THE BEGINNING—

That winter, after my mother lost the baby, she lost her mind. That's the way it seemed to me. After she came home from the hospital she went to her bedroom and slept for two months solid. Just as I feared she was about to become the Rip Van Winkle of Fairvale, I arrived home from school one afternoon and there she was, sitting on the sofa, all wrapped up in her shaggy pink bathrobe, watching TV. She still wasn't much in the mood for talking, though. Whenever I talked to her, whatever I said, she had the same reaction.

"That's nice, dear," she'd say, in a voice thin and flat as glass. Then her eyes would grow cloudy, like milk poured into water. She'd look right past me as if she was studying something on the wall above my head.

By spring she sat long hours at the window watching fresh green shoots, tough as knotted knuckles, punch through frozen earth. Inch by inch by inch by inch, as if it were some prime-time drama on television. But she wouldn't go outside and dig in the dirt like other years. She wouldn't go outside at all.

During those months my father wasn't his great daddy-o-yodelling-fool self either. He wasn't used to doing the laundry or so much cooking for one thing. We managed, but let's just say he's no gourmet cook and we ate enough macaroni and cheese to last me the rest of my life. The food wasn't the worst of it. Picture this teeny-tiny ant at the bottom of the Grand Canyon. That would be me. Our house was hollow.

At night sometimes I heard echoes of a baby crying.

Most likely this was the result of my overactive imagination—something I seem to have been born with. In our family it's spoken of like some sort of hideous birthmark, in a hushed tone. "Oh that's Minn, with her *overactive imagination*." Little do they really know.

The crying I heard seemed real enough to me. More than once, it woke me up, and when I listened in the dark, it stopped. Then there was a happy gurgle like a baby's laugh. I swear that's what I heard, but I guess it doesn't mean it was real. Darkness and sadness can play tricks on people.

Still, it was not my imagination overactive or otherwise that invented the way things were. My father's forehead was like some accordion made of skin, he was so puckered up with worry all the time. My mother was living in some kind of glue bottle. Stuck. I invented new names for her: Watcher of the Growing Grass. Keeper of the Wind Secrets.

And for some reason I couldn't help thinking of the church words I heard once on TV: Blessed fruit of thy womb. The man who said it was wearing a large pointy hat.

I asked Corporal Ray what fruit of thy womb meant. I thought I'd heard fruit of *the loom*, as in underwear. I couldn't understand why a church man would bless underwear.

My father laughed so hard he choked. He gave me a mini anatomy lesson on the word *womb* and a brief version of the story of Mary and Joseph and Jesus. "Fruit of thy womb means a baby," he said finally. "A child."

My mother: with no blessed fruit of her womb.

Except, of course, for me.

— THE WEIRDNESS OF WORDS —

"Your mother lost the baby" is how my father put it the day it happened.

I pictured this cardboard box like the one we had at elementary school for lost mittens and boots and stuff, some sort of lost and found for babies. I wanted to say, "Don't worry, I'm sure she'll find it again."

"It's a miscarriage," he continued, "but to your mother it's the death of our child. Another one. Too many."

Miscarriage. All I could see was my old doll carriage without the doll speeding down a hill towards a baby who *missed* it. The same way you might miss the bus. Nancy Drew and the Mystery of the Missing Stage Coach. I'd read all the Nancy Drew and Trixie Belden mysteries in my mother's cherished collection. I liked Trixie better than Nancy but neither one of them could solve the case of My Mother and the Mystery of the Missing Baby.

Miscarriage. A word like a punch. It was like the wind had just been knocked out of me. See, it wasn't just my mother's loss. For as long as I could remember, I used to pray. I mean, I think it was praying. On my knees, I'd pray with my hands squeezed so tight I made my knuckles white: "Please please please puh-leeze send me a baby brother or sister."

When Corporal Ray said the miscarriage word, we were in the living room. To talk of death in a *living* room? It was the same room they told me about my grandmother dying and so why wasn't it called the dying room or the dead room? Then the room began to come to life. The walls loosened and wobbled, squeezed in on me until there wasn't space in my punched-in belly for an in breath. Something happened then I never saw before and hope to never see again.

My father buried his head in his hands as if hoping I wouldn't see. He began to cry the way little kids cry, gulping air as if he had the hiccups, his shoulders shaking up and down.

My father, Corp. Raymond Hotchkiss of the RCMP, amateur yodelling champion of the world, was bawling like some baby. I blew out my breath. Then I got up to get him a tissue and hugged his head, holding it like it was fragile as an ostrich egg. He didn't blow his nose, honking it on purpose like he always did, to make me laugh. Corporal Ray just kept crying and tearing that tissue into strips and pieces. Until that moment, I never really thought about how *tears* and *tears* were spelled the same.

— ANGELS ON HIGH —

Later that same day we walked to the hospital. The snowbanks were so high it was more like trundling through some marshmallow tunnel. The night was still and the sky blue flannel. It was so cold ice crystals formed inside my nostrils. I pictured miniature stalactites and stalagmites, which made me think of caves. *Minn Hotchkiss and the Cave of Sorrow.*

We stopped in front of the hospital and my father pointed five floors up and three windows across.

"That's your mother's room," he said. "She'll be home tomorrow."

I couldn't help thinking that if my mother had have been there with us she'd be crooning about the colour of the sky. "Winter Blue, perhaps," I could hear her saying. "Indigo Dream." Or maybe just, "Purple Night." The squares of light from those windows would really get her going. "Electric Amber! Topaz

Fluorescent! No, I know, I've got it—Neon Gold!"

It was impossible to me that on such a night as this my mother could be lying in there with no baby.

"Want to go see her?" asked Corporal Ray. His voice left lots of room for saying no.

"Tomorrow," I said, "I'll see her tomorrow." He took my hand. For the first time in ages, I didn't squirm away saying I was too old to hold hands with him. I needed to ask him a question.

Just that afternoon Mrs. Robichaud told me that the baby was an angel in heaven with God now. The Robichauds go to church. They are French and Catholic.

"Dis babee is now one of de purest angels because her feet, dey never even touch da groun, eh?"

That's how I found out the baby would have been a girl. I would have had a sister. Pippa. That was the name we had chosen. Close to Pepper, a spice, like my name. But chosen because of Pippi Longstocking, one of my favourite heroines. A boy would have been Jacob, after Jacob Two-Two.

"And even dough you never see her, her spirit will be wid you always, p'tit poupée." That means *little doll*, Mrs. Robichaud's pet name for me. I liked what she said a lot. Now I had a sister angel. We don't go to church and we're not Catholic. In fact we're not anything but I wished we were. It wasn't the first time.

"Honey, it's not that we're *nothing*," said my mother. This was because I'd printed "nothing" in the blank after *Religion* on a school form in Grade Three. "Put in non-denominational."

"What's that mean?" I asked her.

She thought for a minute. "It's more like we're every-thing," she said. I still leave that blank blank.

I liked Mrs. Robichaud's ideas. I even dared to tell my father exactly what she said and what I thought. That angels were a good thing.

Corporal Ray smiled when I told him and squeezed my hand harder.

"But," I said, "how does anyone know if God and angels are real if we can't see him or her or them or whatever?"

For an answer, my father pointed to the stars.

— STRATEGIES —

There's a good silence, when everything inside you hums—silence like a lullaby you settle down to listen to. That silence is like a blanket you can cuddle under huddled against a windy night. Then there is a kind of silence that sort of drips. Drips like melting icicles. Drip drop drip drop. It makes an ocean that roars so loud you think you could even drown in it. That's what it was like at my house.

I learned to get rid of this kind of silence. There are two ways to do this. Run, run, run. And read, read, read. Yep. You could say these were my lifesaving strategies for overcoming deep-sea silence.

My love of running happened by accident. In fact, until I discovered my hidden gift, my athletic career had been a disaster. I'd never been able to dribble for more than two bounces at a time. I hit my head with the field-hockey stick first time I picked it up. Then there was the time I vaulted over the box horse in gymnastics, drove my knee into my nose and bled all over the floor mat. In Grade Six, I sprained my middle finger trying to volley the volleyball. Picture a cast on a middle finger. At first the teacher thought I was pulling a stunt with a fake cast.

"Take it off," she snapped. "You're not funny."

"I can't," I said, then yelped when she tried to yank it off herself.

Anyhow, run in a straight line? I could do that.

"You have the speed and the flat feet of the sprinter," said Coach Rigby one day in gym class after he'd made us run laps. "I want you on my team, Minn."

He barks when he talks and has a bulldog face. I've never seen so many layers of wrinkles and frowns. He's roly-poly as any stuffed-pillow Santa, with a face as orange as his tracksuit, but apparently he was quite a track star in his heyday. Even for me that's a stretch of the imagination. He's a great guy, though, and I am eternally grateful Coach Rigby noticed my speed and appreciated my flat feet.

Once the spring arrived, every day after school I showed up at practice. And did I run! I ran until my legs burned, ran until my heart thumped double time, ran until my shirt got sweat slickery to my skin, ran until I tasted salt when I licked my lips.

Every day, I ran away from home.

When I got home, it was the reading that saved me from drowning in that sea of silence. Thanks to Mr. Forest, there are more than enough books to choose from in our house. Once a month ever since I can remember he's lugged over this big box crammed full of comics, magazines and novels. He works for a book distributor and brings me the damaged ones that don't sell. Their covers are ripped off.

"They're good books," he says, "even if they don't have the covers. 'Member now, Minn, ya can't judge a book by its cover, eh?" When Mr. Forest laughs, he wheezes. His chest rattles. His belly jiggles. "Seems like I've worked up a thirst bringing over those books." He winks at me.

That's my signal to fetch him a cold beer. Then he plays a game of crib with Corporal Ray. While they're in the kitchen shouting "fifteen two, fifteen four!" I hunker down and crack open the first book. Just the smell of a new book gives me shivers.

He's right about the books being "oldies but goodies." This past winter I read *The Red Badge of Courage*, *Old Yeller*, *Robinson Crusoe*, *The Swiss Family Robinson* and *Treasure Island*.

They're right up there with my mother's old collection of Nancy Drew and Trixie Beldens.

Thanks to Mr. Forest and the books and Coach Rigby and the running, I got through the long Grand Canyon winter and spring. I was pretty sure with the summer coming we would soon be the family we once were.

But my parents had other plans.

— BANISHED —

Right out of a blue-sky morning one day in June at breakfast my father dropped the news.

"We've decided that you should go spend some time with your grandmother when school is through. Only for a month," he said.

My whole universe cracked like the shell of the hard-boiled egg he'd just placed in front of me.

"It's not all summer, only half the summer," he added, as if this halfness would make some difference to me. He sounded like someone had gagged him, stuffed cloth into his mouth so he couldn't talk. Not again, I thought, he's not going to cry again, is he? I still hadn't recovered from the first time.

I am not especially proud of what happened next. I could have said I shall go gladly Father for I am an obedient daughter. I could have said whatever you wish Father perhaps next time you'll ask me first? Instead, I scraped my chair back from the table and screamed "*I'm not going!*" up every step to my room. There are twenty-one plus the landing. I didn't slam the door but cried so loud I hoped my sobs would sink right through the floor into the hardness of my father's heart. Then I tried to bargain. Not with my earthly father.

On my knees, I prayed. At least I think it was praying. Loudly. "Please if I do not have to go to Boulder Basin I promise when I grow up I will be a missionary and help starving children in Third World countries, the ones with milk like dry chalk around their mouths, their eyes black pools of need, their bellies swollen with hunger."

"Cut the melodrama, Cinnamon! You're going. That's final!"

I went to the top of the stairs and yelled back down at him, "What about my running? What about my track?"

"I've already talked to your coach. He's drawing up a schedule. You can run just as easily in Boulder Basin. You'll be back in time for the provincials." But this time his voice sounded less sure. That's when I slammed the door.

"Cucurbita maxima!" I screamed at the top of my lungs. Translation: big pumpkin! I am only allowed to curse using the Latin names of plants. This was my mother's idea after I repeated something Corporal Ray said when he banged his thumb with a hammer when I was three. I am also allowed to use geographical place names. Kalamazoo! Tatamagouche! Shawinigan! This is something I refrain from doing, however, as it is an irritating habit of my grandmother's. My grandmother, the retired history and geography teacher, still loves giving little pop quizzes even in moments of anger or excitement.

My cussing got no reaction from my father. I shouted louder.

"Cnicus benedictus!" The *c* is silent. Translation: bitter thistle weed! Still nothing.

"Ni-PISS-i-quit!" I hollered next. Nipisiquit is in northern New Brunswick.

That did it. My father leapt up the stairs two at a time and barged into my room. As I hightailed it onto my bed he lifted his foot. To boot me in the butt, I think.

My father, who never ever hits, struck his toe on the metal mattress frame.

He yelped. He forgot the Latin-plant cursing rule and all his geography lessons. He shouted out the Lord's name in vain as well as a few other words that would have been bleeped out on TV. He hopped around on one foot, held the other foot in his hands. That's when my mother appeared with her crumpled bed face.

She was pale and as see-through as the last sliver of a bar of soap. Strange sounds came from an *o* in her mouth—mouse squeaking sounds. Her shoulders were shaking up and down and her head jerked back like she was taking some kind of seizure. She was, wonder of wonders, *laughing*. I mean really laughing.

My father froze. Then, in slow motion, he floated towards her, wrapped his arms around her and began to laugh himself. My mother poked her head out from underneath his armpit. She was framed perfectly in the triangle of his arm.

"Madonna," she said to me. (That's the name she's always called me whenever I made a scene, or Pre Madonna when she's really ticked off. I hadn't heard it for months.) "Madonna, you're not going to win any Academy Awards in this house for . . . ," she broke off for another fit of laughter, "for a performance like that one! Your father and I need some time alone. We've things to do, like . . ."

Her voice broke then, like a twig snapped clean in two. "Like empty . . . out the baby's room." The laughter was over.

"The thought of you going to your grandmother's this year is more than I can bear. But she's old, she's family, and we need you to do this for us."

I nodded. Maybe because it was the first time she said more than one whole sentence in a month. Maybe because it made me think that there was hope things might have a chance of being normal again. Mostly, though, it was the guilt that made me cave in. They'd never said a thing to me, but I knew.

Everything was my fault. The baby dying and my mother the zombie and my father the troubling gourmet.

"I'll go" is all I said.

What I was thinking is anything, *anything, anything,* if it means you coming back from this ocean of silence we've all been drowning in. If you and Corporal Ray will keep laughing together. Just like this.

Dad went to get the poor toe x-rayed. I can't help it. I still have to laugh remembering the look on his face that day as he hopped around my room like some one-legged kangaroo.

I'll always be able to say the first and only time my father raised a hand to me, he raised a foot instead. And broke his toe. He does a much better job catching the bad guys.

— WITH FRIENDS LIKE CAROLINA —

For my parents' sake, I pretended everything was tickety-boo. This is an expression my mother used to use a lot—before she forgot how to smile. Before she lost her voice. When she used to care about what I felt. I saved my complaining for Carolina. Carolina Jenkins is my best friend.

"And who would ever thunk it?" she loves to remind me. We didn't exactly get off to a great start. We were only six, after all.

"Her name is Carolina." My mother told me that as I was chasing an O around my bowl of alphabet cereal. So how would I ever be friends with a girl named Carolina, a name that tripped off my tongue like a song? Besides her name having four syllables and mine having only three, a difference that made all the difference in the world, was her skirt.

"Nova Scotia tartan—that's what that is," said my

mother, "and why don't you wear that jumper your grand-mother gave you last Christmas more often?" Fat chance.

And her shoes. Carolina that new girl who moved in next door had black patent-leather shoes with bows in the middle and never, not even for special, was I allowed shoes like that. On account of my flat feet. Instead, I had to wear brown lace-up lock-your-feet-in shoes—Oxfords is what they were called. Ugly is what they were.

"So go on over there after breakfast, just go over there, dear, and make friends," said my mother. Just like that.

The houses on our street are exactly the same, like shoeboxes made of brick. The veranda railings almost touch, so I didn't have to go next door to meet her. I just plunked myself down on our back steps and started peeling the paint, getting warm yellow slivers under-neath my nails, sticky as gum. Carolina was sitting on her back steps playing with dolls. We were almost in spitting distance of each other.

"Take a picture why don't you?" she yelled and stuck out her tongue. I was just about to go back inside when her back door wheezed open. A boy, her brother I sup-posed it was, came out and thumped her a good one on the head. She ran after him, tackled him like a pro wrestler, jumped up and down on him and threw him around like he was some old sack of potatoes. Then an upstairs window scritched open and a voice sharp as thistles cut through everything.

"You two hooligans stop that this minute! I leave you alone for two minutes and look what happens! Git in here, I said *git* in here, this minute!"

Carolina looked over at me. "I said take a picture, fart face," she said. Then stuck out her tongue.

I skedaddled into our house to tell my mother what happened, especially about the swearing I heard. The f-word.

My mother acted as if it was no big deal. In fact, I am sure I caught her trying to smother a laugh. Later that afternoon we baked chocolate chip cookies and invited the Jenkinses over for tea. Carolina was putting on her best manners for my mother.

"Thank you, Mrs. Hotchkiss," she said, and then when my mother's back was turned she made a face at me. I made one back—my best face, the one where I can cross my eyes and stick my tongue almost to the tip of my nose. She liked it, I guess, because she laughed. I told her I liked her shoes. "Wanna try them on?" she asked. That was all it took. Friends forever!

Our mothers never did become too chummy. I guess they had too many differences. For example, my mother wears a terrycloth housecoat with bacon grease always spattered on the collar and Carolina's mother wears a pink see-through thingy that reminds me of cotton candy. My mother's a scrubaholic. Carolina's mother lets her keep rabbits in the living room. She never mentions the rabbit turds scattered like raisins over their carpet.

After I complained to Carolina about being shipped off to Boulder Basin, she stood in my bedroom, with her hands on her hips. She takes being three months older than me very seriously.

"So then, here's what you're going to do. One: you're going to go practise running so you can come back here and be track star extraordinaire in the August meet. Two: you are going to do detective work. Find out if Hardly Whynot really does have a summer home in Boulder Basin and is living incognito. That means in disguise. You can get his autograph and cheer up your depressing—I mean depressed mother. Three: you can write me letters. Don't get me wrong, I'll miss you loads, but you're going to be fine just fine."

"But you don't know my grandmother!"

She squeezed my hand. "Maybe you don't either," she said.

"What's with you?" I snarled.

"I can't believe she's as witchy as you say."

"She is! A sour old Vinegar Witch."

"Least you have a grandmother—I don't. Maybe I could come down for a visit. In the meantime," she giggled, "I'll try to keep the other girls away from Gavin."

She poked me in the ribs and started chanting, "Gavin and Minn, up in a tree . . ." Made me furious.

Gavin is not important to my story. Gavin Williamson was a long-distance runner. I was a sprinter. We trained together all spring. When he smiled his teeth were as polished as Chiclets. His skin was the colour of coffee with double cream. He smelled like herbal shampoo. When I told him I was leaving for most of the summer all he said was, "Bummer."

"It's a sign," said Carolina, "that the feeling between you two is mutual."

"I couldn't care less," I said.

"That's a double negative and a lie as big as Australia," she replied.

"I have other more important things to think about," I said to her.

She giggled. "What's more important than l-u-v?"

My father says that Carolina is boy crazy. He hopes I'll always be able to keep my head on straight when it comes to boys. I'm embarrassed for him whenever he tries to talk about stuff like that. It's as if it's a foreign language or something. He stutters and stammers and can't quite put a sentence together. Still, I have to admit, he was better than my mother, who still wasn't even trying to talk to me at that time, in any language.

— EVERYWHERE A PIPPA —

My mother wasn't the only one with problems. I noticed that the world was suddenly filled with sisters. There they were, holding hands in line at the supermarket, dressed in matching outfits. There they were, shopping in the mall. Hand in hand, sisters walked to school together. I saw them on TV brushing each other's hair and trading beauty secrets. In one show, two sisters had a huge fight over some boy but hugged and made up in the end.

Sisters ate from the same box of large fries at McDonald's. They cheered for each other at basketball games. Sisters were maids of honour at weddings and fairy godmother aunts. Sisters were also Catholic nuns.

The word *sister* echoed in other words: transistor, persister, resister. It rhymed with mister and blister and twister. And that's how I felt. As if I'd been burned and blistered. Everything was twisted upside down and backwards. We were supposed to have had a birth in our family. Instead we had death. My parents were ghosts of the people they used to be.

Ashes to ashes, dust to dust. That's all my mother did. Dust her china cabinet and play sucky songs by Hardly Whynot. Hardly? Hardly my mother. And there I was, doing my homework and the laundry and the dishes. Night after night. All this after trying to swallow Corporal Ray's nightly concoctions. His so-called suppers were more disastrous than mine.

"It tastes worse than dog food," I told Carolina.

"Yuck." She didn't ask how would you know unless you've eaten dog food—like a normal person might. That's because we tried some once when we were seven. "Really yuck," she repeated.

I love it when someone understands.

— CONFESSION —

Sometimes growing up
feels a lot like throwing up.

That's the best, the shortest and the only poem I ever wrote. It summed up how I felt exactly.

"Good use of graphic detail and evocative use of simile," wrote Miss Armstrong-Blanchett on my final test. Although her name is half French she was my English teacher. In winter, she wore a calf-length navy blue skirt with different coloured turtlenecks that matched her tights. Every spring she blossomed into a flower. She wore gauzy dresses that flowed to her ankles. She didn't walk, she glided across the room like a ballerina, saying things like *that was a cliché, I know you can be more original, think deeper.* Her hair was super short and never the same colour more than a month. Her earrings were miniature mobiles.

When Miss Armstrong-Blanchett talked, words danced from her lips. Ono-mat-o-pee-a. Sir Charles G.D. Roberts. I think she knew we all said the G.D. stood for God dam because it was a bonus question on the exam. I wrote in George Douglas and got my A plus.

Miss Armstrong-Blanchett called me in to her class just before school was out and asked me if there was anything I needed to talk about.

"No, but thanks for asking," I said. I squirmed. She had a stare that could burn right through to the inside of me.

"I was intrigued by the metaphors on your exam," she continued. Just as I thought. She liked the throwing up one, so I knew which one she meant. "'My mother is a bleached-out dishrag full of holes'? I wouldn't read too much into it."

"So your mother's okay?"

I was very close to saying no, she's not, in fact she's gone missing and doesn't seem to know or care I am alive. But I just looked at the floor. It was stifling hot in the room. Someone down the hall started pounding on the piano.

"And the other one. The extended metaphor?" she said finally.

I frowned as if I couldn't recall it.

"'The heart has four chambers: isolation chamber, torture chamber, chamber of horrors and chamber of ghosts.'" She had it memorized?

"I was under pressure," I said. "I just wrote the first thing that popped into my head."

"I know. That's why we're talking."

"I've got what my folks call an overactive imagination."

"Overactive? I don't know about that. Compared to whom? Maybe it's just *your* imagination. A poetic imagination."

I think it was supposed to be compliment but I wasn't sure. Especially when she said what she did next.

"When you were little, did you ever have an imaginary friend?"

I gawked at her. "No!" I tried to sound insulted. It was also a big lie. I had Orangey. Orangey was a teeny-tiny elephant who went everywhere with me. Orangey listened when I talked and often talked while I listened. Of course I'd outgrown Orangey. Years ago.

"Too bad," she went on. "I did. I had a fairy named Flower."

How cliché, I know you can be more original, I wanted to say. Instead, I smiled at her as if she were a silly child. I so did not want to know the secret fantasy life of my English teacher.

She handed me a blue spiral book with a happy-faced moon on it.

"It's not more homework." She smiled. A rare occurrence. "It's the best kind of book for someone like you.

It's filled with blank pages. You can always talk to the page." I didn't know what to say. Thanks, Miss Armstrong-Blanchett, I'll miss your lime-green outfit the most? And what did she mean, *someone like me?*

"I appreciate this," I said as I got up to leave. "Have a good summer," I added over my shoulder.

Truth is, Miss Armstrong-Blanchett read me like . . . well, yes, like an open book. The thoughts of toodling off to Boulder Basin to spend the summer with my grandmother did make me almost sick to my stomach.

My father's mother is a bow-legged stubborn witch with chin hairs that sprout from a mole the colour and shape of a kidney bean. That's for starters. Our problematic history goes back a long way.

First off, my father's father, Emerson Hotchkiss, died long before I was born, and the witch remarried a man by the name of Hennigar. He died before I was born too, but she had taken his name. I could never say Hennigar, so I called her Nana Vinegar. That never pleased her, as you can imagine. But it fit her perfectly, she was such a sour old thing.

Things really came to a head between us during what I call the Night of the Jellied Tongue. I was eight. My grandmother cooked tongue of beef and made me eat it. That's right, *tongue* of beef. There it was, one big pink tongue on a platter in the middle of the dining-room table. Now, if you have ever seen tongue of beef, you would know that you could see the ridges and furrows and little spongy thingamajiggies just like when you look at your own tongue in the mirror. It's disgusting. I pictured some cow, one who could no longer moo, who could no longer chew its cud, wandering around the pasture, tongueless. I was ready for the tongue to spring from the table and go looking for its owner.

"I won't eat that!" I screamed, surprising myself at how loud and screechy my voice was, like someone playing bad violin.

"Now, Minn, dear, your nana's gone to a lot of trouble," my mother said, smiling through clenched teeth at the witch. Then she hissed to me under her breath, like some ventriloquist not even moving her lips. "Puhleeze, Minn, *not* the very first night?"

My grandmother gave me one of her ferocious shaggy-eyebrowed frowns. So I tried. Really, I tried.

I put that tongue on my tongue.

I chewed.

I spit it out into my napkin.

Worse than looking at tongue of beef is looking at half-chewed tongue of beef.

My grandmother sent me to bed without supper.

This is really the reason I did what I did the next day, which is really the reason I knew from that day onwards that my grandmother no longer loved me, if she ever had at all.

In the evening, when I was sure all the relatives were having their tea after supper, I took an old mop, braided the strands into pigtails and tied them with my red ribbons. Then I padded it with pillows, tied it with stockings and dressed it in my clothes. I climbed up the outside steps to the balcony at the back of the house. The balcony is directly above the dining room and the dining room has a picture window overlooking the sea. Looking out at the sunset, after supper with tea, is an evening ritual.

So when I knew they'd all be gazing out the window oohing and aahing and saying one more time how the colour was like the inside of a cantaloupe or they'd never seen a sky so purple, I threw the mop over the balcony and screamed an impressively believable blood-curdling scream.

They saw what looked like my body whiz by to her death on the rocks below. I watched from the balcony as they rushed outside and ran to the rocks. I was lying on my bed reading my grandmother's Bible when Corporal Ray burst in.

"You could have given your grandmother a heart attack!" my father said to me, and more than his voice was shaking. He pulled me off the bed.

"You are coming down to apologize right now." He steered me by my collar all the way to the dining room.

"Look what you did to your poor mother!"

Someone was putting a cloth on my mother's forehead and giving her whisky.

All my grandmother said to me that night, her face so close to mine I could have bitten off those three chin hairs, was this: "I have never ever known a child to harbour such hatred in her heart." This was much worse than "Pugwash!" One of her favourites when she was displeased.

Harbour. I thought the word was a noun up until then. A place where boats anchored and little houses like crooked rows of teeth painted happy colours lined the shore, where dinghies bobbed up and down on waves and lobster traps were stacked atop each other, stinking in the sun. Harbour, a safe place to stay out of the wind.

Yes, I had a harbour of hate in my heart. And she knew it. So let's say we've never been on the best of terms since then.

Summer would be torture, I told Carolina.

"You are so melodramatic," she said. "Get a grip."

"My life is a *disaster*. A total *disaster*," I wailed.

I realize, now, I didn't know the meaning of the word.

≋ The Announcement ≋

I was born in Ashton-under-Lyne, Lancashire County,
England in eighteen hundred and sixty-one, the youngest
son of Patrick and Mary Hindley and the baby brother of
Bridget, Lucy and Thomas. My father emigrated from
Ireland during the potato famine and found work at one
of the cotton mills. Shortly thereafter, he met one Mary
Cook of Stalybridge. "Black rot was the reason I came to
England," he loved to say, "and your mother's the reason
I stayed."

After the birth of my sisters, they moved into one of the
brick row houses owned by the mill. It was the house I was
born into, and the place I'd always known as home. But on
the evening of March the eighth, 1873, our family's destiny
changed forever.

≋

Ashton-under-Lyne, 1873

"Can't we eat supper without him?" Thomas was three years older and a head taller than me. And whining like some big baby. "I'm starving," he grumbled.

Lovesick was more like it. Soon as he'd slopped up the last bit of supper, belched, brushed his teeth and combed his hair, he'd be off like some panting puppy. Lickety-split, up the road, two lanes over to a red-brick row house identical to ours he'd run, straight into the waiting arms of his girl, Rebecca. My big brother, a regular Romeo! Lot of bother, if you asked me. Then again, I was only twelve. According to Thomas, it was just a matter of time before I understood real passion. *Pa-shun.* Sounded to me like a rash you caught that made you itchy. Since he'd been seeing her, he was nothing but a pain and twitch.

"Mum?"

Our mother was peering out the window, lost in a heap of worry.

"Where have you got to now, Patrick Hindley?" she muttered.

"*Mu-um?*" Thomas looked at me in exasperation. "Do you think she even hears me?"

I shrugged.

"I heard all right, and you know better. Eat supper without your father? Not in this house."

Thomas groaned and began drumming his fingers on the tabletop.

"Let off!" I said. "I'm trying to write neat as I can."

He drummed louder and faster.

Mum rapped his shoulder with the ladle. "For heaven's sake, Tom, get up here and make yourself useful. Stir the stew!" She pushed him to the stove.

When she turned back to the window he imitated her frown so perfectly I burst out laughing.

"And what's so funny?" she snapped at me.

"Nothing, Mum. Sorry, Mum!"

"Get your head back in those books, then, or you'll be sorrier still whereonearthisthatman?"

Sometimes Mum talked whole nights without taking a breath.

"Ow!" It was Thomas.

"Serves you right," said Mum without even looking over her shoulder. "For making fun of your mother and sneaking a taste."

She really did have a second set of eyes in the back of her head.

Thomas's eyes watered with pain.

"Oh poor Tom-tom," I teased. "Maybe Becca will kiss it better." I made loud smooching sounds. He looked ready to throttle me.

"Back to the books," Mum ordered, but giggled despite herself. "Thomas, your face is as red as those embers in the fire. And John, some fine day it'll be you."

"Not likely," I muttered.

"The stew's burning, I think. Maybe we should eat it?"

Thomas was persistent; I'll give him that.

Mum shooed him away from the stove and he sat back down beside me.

"Suppose Dad's at the pub? We left the mill together and he *was* acting kind of strange," he whispered.

I shook my head. Our father was not a drinker. Besides, I knew where he was. But I'd been sworn to secrecy.

"Then where could he be?" Thomas leaned in closer. "There's been some trouble at the mill, you know. Talk of strikes."

"It's okay, Tom. Really, it is," I said.

"You know where he's got to, don't you?"

I nodded but held my finger up to my lips. "It's a surprise," I wrote out and slid the paper over to him.

A thumping of feet at the door then, and Dad burst in the room like a gust of wind. He smelled like clean night air mixed with tobacco and ale. Mum sniffed the air suspiciously. She arched one eyebrow and put her hand on her hip.

"He *has* been drinking," hissed Thomas.

Dad's eyes were full of fun, his cheeks as red as if he'd just been slapped. When he took off his hat, his thick black hair stood on end like a rooster's comb. Mum reached out, smoothed it down and smothered the urge to laugh. His voice blared like a trumpet.

"Look, Mare, I did it! Look here, one-way tickets for us all!" He started to sing in his deep Irish off-key voice as he jigged towards her.

Thomas sat bolt upright. "What's that again?"

Mum's mouth opened in a tiny startled circle. She dropped the crockery pot filled with stew and it smashed on the stone floor.

Ignoring the mess, Dad wrapped his arms around Mum. He danced her around the room.

"Patrick Hindley! You're not kidding this time, are you? It's for real? We're going to see my girls? Tell me I'm not dreaming."

He pinched her on the bottom "You're not dreaming, Mare." He spun her again, hugged her close.

I started mopping up the mess for something to do. Thomas was holding his head in his hands.

Our parents continued to rock back and forth as if we were invisible.

"Your girls, Mare, and your grandkids too." Mum was sniffling by that time. Dad stroked her hair, like she was a dog needing petting. He winked at us over the top of her head.

"We'll be leaving in a fortnight," Dad said. "It's not a lot of time. Will we be ready, boys?"

"Yes, sir," I said, grinning from ear to ear.

Thomas said nothing.

"Tom?"

We all waited.

"Yes, but—," said Thomas.

Thomas was thinking about Becca? At a time like this? Well, too bad for him, I thought.

Ever since our sisters had married and sailed across the sea, ever since they started sending those letters filled with excitement about the sights of New York, I'd been dreaming of joining them. New World, new life. Our mother missed her daughters something fierce. She'd weep for no reason, knit her brow as tightly as the bonnets she was making—"for my grandchildren who I'll never ever ever *ever* see," she'd say. And her sigh would last longer than a month.

My father finally made the decision to join them. "Family's meant to be together," he'd told me when he confided his plans.

"John, catch me, catch me, catch me can!" he shouted then.

"Patrick, he's too heavy and you're too old," Mum started in. Too late. I ran across the room, jumped into outstretched arms and wrapped my legs around my father's waist. It was a game we'd played since I was a tot. He step-danced with me attached like a raggedy doll, hanging upside down.

"Look here, Mare, the boy's so big now, his hair can sweep up the floor for us!"

Next thing I knew Dad was dumping me down like one of his sacks of cotton at the mill. He threw Thomas on top and hugged us in. Mum didn't get away either.

"Imagine," she said, gasping for breath. "Imagine if some-one could see in this place now, what a bunch of raving fools they'd think we must be."

Thomas wriggled out from under the pile.

"Tom?" Dad's smile crumpled into an awkward lopsided grin. "Tom?"

"Got some thinking to do, if that's okay with you. Got to think over whether I'll be sailing with you."

Silence followed.

"You're old enough to make the right decision," Dad replied.

I watched Tom pull on his coat and walk out the door.

"Gurls," I said to my folks. "Nothing but a whole heap of trouble."

My parents exchanged worried glances.

My hunger was gone, replaced by what felt like a lump of coal in my belly. Sure, Thomas wasn't perfect, but I couldn't imagine not having my big brother by my side.

⪼ Preparations ⪻

"For folks that got nothing, we sure got a lot," said Thomas.

Mum wiped the sweat from her brow with the sleeve of one of Dad's old shirts. Then she bit into the shirt to make a tear and ripped it in three. She tossed two rags at us and dipped her piece in a pail of sudsy water.

"We're not leaving this place dirty," she warned us. "No one's going to say the Hindleys left filth behind for someone else to mop up. Scrub!"

She was thinking of the Grovers, who moved away the year before. People still talked about the smell of rotten eggs they left for the new tenants to try to get rid of.

"Once folks leave this town, those left behind don't have a good word to say about them anyhow, Mum. They're all wanting to get out of the mill and are just plain jealous when some folks do. Don't fuss."

Thomas should have known better. "Scrub!" repeated Mum.

All around the room our belongings were stacked in piles.

Things to go to family and friends, things to go to St.
Michael's parish for folks with less, things we were taking with
us. Simple enough. But simple does not mean easy. Not at all.

"Feels like I'm throwing away bits of myself," muttered
Mum. Mostly we were down to linens and dishes and a few
books, including the Bible.

"I brought it with me from Ireland," Dad said, "when I
was about the same age Thomas is now."

"There isn't a hope" Mum snapped, "that a lifetime is
going to fit into two wooden crates."

It seemed the closer we were getting to leaving, the
crosser she was getting.

"That's the point, Mare," Dad said patiently. "They're
only *things*. We have a new life ahead, so we take only what
is absolutely necessary of the old life. We'll get what we
need when we get there."

Mum snorted and disappeared into their bedroom. A
few minutes later a scraping sound made us wince as she
hauled a cradle out into the middle of the room.

"Now, about this, then."

"Now that, I was thinking, could fetch me a good price."

"Patrick, you made that cradle with your bare hands
practically and hardly a tool save a saw, a hammer and a
knife. Look at that carving! You'll never get what it's worth.
Besides, my babies were rocked to sleep in that cradle and
now I'm going to rock my grandkids in it. Yes, I am."

"Mare, there's no room. Two crates, I said."

"If it's money that's the problem, fine. One crate then, and this strapped to the top of that."

He sighed. "All right. One crate and the cradle."

Thomas and I exchanged amused glances.

That was the end of their squabble. As always, Dad put up the best argument he could but Mum won him over to her way of thinking. I never heard them fight fierce, not like my chum Michael's folks. Underneath their angry words was hate, you could tell. Hindley folks didn't know about that kind of wounding. Sometimes Michael didn't even go home nights. I couldn't imagine that.

Unlike Thomas. He had no sense of family loyalty from what I could tell. He was acting like some traitor in my eyes. He was still torn between coming and going. And he was hardly home.

"Where you going now?" I'd ask.

"Out," he'd say. Or, "Mind your business." Or just slam the door.

I spent my last evenings in Ashton-under-Lyne gathering memories. I shuffled past the row houses in our neighbourhood, peeking in the amber windows where families were snuggled in. The sounds of laughter and even quarrels tugged at me. It would be strange leaving. I glimpsed Tom from time to time on these outings, but he didn't see me. He was otherwise occupied, you might say. He walked arm in arm with Rebecca, her head against his shoulder. He stayed out a lot later than me. He often could not sleep and began a strange sort of ritual. He'd get up after tossing and turning about and go out for long runs all the way to Lord's fields he told me. He'd come back, breathless, his lungs still bursting from the cold March air.

"Let him be," I heard Mum warn Dad one night. "He's just chasing after his heart's truth."

"A new life in a new city with your folks and your brother? What's more important than that?" I asked one night when he woke me up getting into his bed.

"She cried."

"What's that?"

"Rebecca cried when I told her. Cried until the collar of my shirt was soaked with her tears."

"You going to let a few tears lock you in this place forever?"

But the picture was disturbing, even to me. Rebecca was bright eyed and cherub faced. And always smiling—especially around Thomas.

Thomas seemed to read my thoughts.

"She's got a smile that could crack your heart wide open." He sighed. "A new life without Becca would be like a sunrise without sun."

I groaned. "I thought I was supposed to be the poetic one."

"Shut your mouth," he said. In our house, that expression was worse than cussing.

I did feel some for him. How was a person to ever know when a decision was the right one or the wrong one? Especially if it meant leaving someone you loved?

By that time I knew Thomas had more than an itchy rash.

≈ Persuasions ≈

"I'd trade places with Thomas in a second," said Michael. "Sure wish I was going."

"Me, too." Silence hung between us heavier than a soggy blanket on a line.

"Maybe you could be a stowaway," I suggested. This was something I had proposed to Thomas—that we could sneak Rebecca onto the ship somehow.

"Are you living on the moon?" he'd snapped. "Cracked in the head? There are rats as big as Dad on a ship like that for one thing."

"Sorry," I said. "I was only trying to help." I was also being as sugary nice as I could at every possible moment. "Why don't you go on over and see her. I don't mind doing your scrubbing." He was off like he was on fire. No thank you, of course, but he did give me a playful cuff on the side of my head.

Michael, though? He perked right up at my idea. "A stowaway! Maybe I could," he said.

"Really? I should tell you about the rats . . ."

"Rats? My dad's the rat. I'd go, but I couldn't leave my mum to be alone with that bugger." He spit on the ground. "Some day, though, I'll join you, right?"

"Right." Even to my own ears, my voice lacked conviction.

We sat on the bank of the canal, skipped some rocks and threw sticks in the river, watching them swirl around and be carried off.

To just get on that train to Liverpool! All the packing and sorting and scrubbing and saying goodbye was exhausting. Even I began to wonder whether sailing to a new life was a good thing or not. I hated the waiting. My mother did too, though she kept telling me to have patience. "It's a virtue," she reminded me. Well, I wasn't very virtuous. Besides, every moment that went by, I felt my chances of getting Thomas to come with us were slipping away. He was still droopy eyed as a cocker spaniel and so *silent*.

I went to my parents. They were sympathetic but no help, really. They told me it was his business. I noticed, however, that my mother was cooking all his favourite meals.

So I came up with another plan. I decided it was time to use the powers of persuasion my teachers told me I possessed. I waited until we were side by side in our beds a few nights before our leaving date.

"Thomas?"

"What?"

"You coming with us or what?"

"Go to sleep."

"Tom?"

"What is it?"

"When you going to know your mind?"

"I know my mind."

"You're staying?"

Silence. Almost breathless, I plunged in.

"Thing is, I've been thinking this through."

"You have, have you?"

"I have."

"And?"

"Here's what I think I'd do."

"You never even kissed a girl."

"Doesn't mean I can't think. In fact, seems to me my thinking's not as muddy as yours."

"Muddy?"

"All dirtied up with the scum of love."

Thomas laughed. "Where on earth do you get those expressions of yours? But truth of it is, I don't know what to think."

I swallowed the lump in my throat.

"You come with us, see? Get work at the tannery with our brother-in-laws. Gareth and Simon would put in a good word for you, right? Save your money, send for Rebecca, get married and live right next door to me."

Thomas laughed and stifled a yawn. "Live next door to you?"

"Well, figure you'll need your privacy some."

"Why would we live next door to you, then?"

"That way," I continued, "I can watch your wee ones for you."

The pillow hit me square in the face.

"Go to sleep John."

"I can't."

"Recite me one of them poems from all that learning of yours."

"Really?"

"Yeah. Always puts *me* to sleep right away."

I threw the pillow back and cleared my throat.

> "A brother's best friend is his brother,
> Indeed he's his chum for life.
> For a man needs to let go his mother,
> And a brother's more fun than a wife."

Thomas chuckled. "One of yours?"

"Penned especially for the occasion," I confessed.

"Cut the ruckus, boys," yelled Dad from below. "Or the Black Knight will get ya!"

Thomas snickered. No matter how old we got, our father still thought stories of the Black Knight could scare us. The Black Knight was said to prowl the streets of Ashton after dark ready to snatch naughty children. I had more than my share of nightmares when I was younger. Once I imagined I heard the clang of his suit of armour outside the window. I screamed for Mum. But it was only Thomas, banging on a pot. He got in big trouble for that one. But he was scaring me more with all his silence and indecision.

"And besides . . . if you stay in Ashton . . . ," I began.

"What of it?"

"I'll be all alone."

And that was *my* heart's truth.

He didn't say a word in reply.

Black Knight? Black night. We turned our backs to each other. It was a long time before either one of us slept.

The day before we left, he handed me a book. *Around the World in Eighty Days, by Mr. Jules Verne,* I read.

"I figure it'll keep you company," Thomas said.

It must have cost him every shilling he ever saved. I'd never owned a real new book before.

"You're supposed to open it in the middle first," he said. "That way pages won't fall out."

I did. The book cracked with newness. Then I turned to the front.

Thomas was never one for proper writing but I could still make out his message. Only too well.

> *Happy sailing!*
> *Your big brother—*
> *Always,*
> *Thomas*

— TRAVELLING SHOW —

The bus trip was like taking a bath in diesel fuel. It was a five-hour trip on the Acadia Bus Lines, and we stopped at just about every Tim Hortons along the way. I had so many Timbits, my stomach was sugar coated. I popped the Gravol that Corporal Ray had given me just in case. It made me drowsy but I couldn't seem to get comfortable enough to sleep. Instead, I watched the clouds reflected in the window. It was as if the entire sky had flooded the window and changed it the bright blue of a computer screen. The clouds were chalky. If I were to reach out my hand, I was sure I could rub them away. "Cirrus, cumulus, stratus," I chanted to myself in a whisper. Cirrus. Cumulus. Stratus. Words that made me feel as if I was talking in another language. Almost like praying. Usually I forgot what kind of cloud was which and it never mattered much to me before, but now it did. Clouds had taken on a whole new meaning for me.

Pippa, when she visited, only once—in a dream—was on a cloud.

"The stars at night and the clouds by day," my father told me that night after the God question. "That's how I feel close to those I've lost. Remember that, too, Minn. When in doubt, or feeling alone or afraid, lift up your eyes to the sky."

I'm not sure I've ever felt lonelier in my life as I did that whole bus trip. I was being sent away from those I loved. Banished. Exiled. Afraid? Well, my O.I. was kicking in again. Sometimes an overactive imagination can be damaging to your mental health. The man across the aisle from me looked like a newly released convict ready to go back to his hometown to seek revenge. He'd been guzzling liquor out of a brown paper bag the whole time. You could smell it plain as anything. Around Londonderry, he started up singing to himself. After he nodded off to sleep, his head began bumping against the windowpane, leaving grease smudges all over. Spittle dribbled down his chin like baby drool. I felt sorry for him more than afraid. Still, I wouldn't look him in the eye when he woke up. I knew better. Corporal Ray had warned me about talking to strangers. This buddy was a strange one for sure.

I plugged into my Walkman. It was a gift from my parents before I left.

"Good for training," said my father. My mother

handed me a boxed set of the Ladybugs' greatest hits. Not my taste, but better than the hum of the motor.

I was grateful for the noisy three-year-old who had been playing peek-a-boo with me the whole trip. She was wearing a hat with a rubber dinosaur on top. Its jaws snapped open and shut every time she moved her head. A laughing dinosaur. What will they think of next? Just an hour outside of the basin, she worked up enough nerve to come and crawl up in the seat beside me.

"Honey, get down, don't bother the nice girl," said her mother, who looked like those women in postcards of the Swiss Alps, a woman someone might call Fraulein. Maybe because she called me a nice girl, I piped up right away.

"She's no bother," I said.

"Okay," shrugged Fraulein, "but I warn you, she's a talker."

That turned out to be the understatement of the decade. Her name was Abby. For some reason, this rhyme started up in my head: *Gabby Abby talked so much, she talked of this and that and such.* That's all I could get to because she kept interrupting me.

"What's dat?" she said.

"My key chain," I replied.

"What's dat?" she said.

"A book I'm reading," I told her.

"What are dose?" she giggled and poked two fingers right in my ..."Boobies!" she squealed. "Boobies boobies!"

I wanted to choke her. I was sure every person on the bus must have heard.

"Shh!" I hissed. The way she looked at me then, all pouts and with her eyes as innocent as could be and then whispering "Booby" one more time, cracked me up. "Here," I said. "Want some chocolate milk?"

I rummaged in my knapsack and found my last carton and a straw. When she got to the bottom she did that straw-sucking thing kids do.

"I sink it's all gone," she wailed. "I sink it's all gone."

"Was it good?" I asked.

"Dee-licioush! Any more?"

"Sorry, that's all," I said. "I like your hat," I added, hoping to change the topic. She took it off and put it on my head and then snuggled right beside me with her book.

"Read," she said.

So I did. I sat there on that bus with a dinosaur hat on my head and read *Go Dog Go* until she fell sound asleep. Her hair smelled of baby shampoo, and her breath, despite the chocolate milk, was more like apple juice and barbecue potato chips.

"Boulder Basin," the driver announced over his microphone. "Ten-minute stop."

When I went to get my duffel bag from the luggage compartment, I heard a thumping above my head. There was Gabby Abby squishing her face against the window as if kissing me. I blew her a kiss and turned away. I had what my mother used to call a sad throat. It's the feeling you get when you watch a really sad movie or just before you are going to cry. Sometimes a sad throat means tears. Other times, you just have to swallow hard and it will pass. I swallowed. Still, it had happened.

For just a second, I couldn't help wondering what Pippa would have looked like at three.

— THE WELCOME WITCH —

Boulder Basin is not what you could even call a village. It's just a strip of road that forms a semicircle around the harbour. There's a wharf, a straggle of houses, a post office, a small fish-and-chips restaurant and Harv's.

Nana was deep in conversation with Harvey himself. Harv Jollymore of Harvey's Fuel-Up and General Store must be at least six foot five. That's a giant around Boulder Basin. For some reason, they seem to make all the men around there old and small. Harvey's not young himself, his hair the creamy white of vanilla ice cream and his face creased like an old map that's been folded and unfolded in all the wrong places. The thing about Harv I always remembered from when I was younger was his hands. They were big, all right, like the rest of him, but it was his fingers that amazed me the most. They reminded me of those large fat cigars Corporal Ray smokes at New Year's, and stained that colour too.

They looked like they had been dipped in tar that just wouldn't come off. Even in church on Sundays, you could tell he'd scrubbed and scrubbed. I guess you just can't get grease off a mechanic's hands. Harv saw me before the witch did.

"Well look here, when'd you go and grow up? Makes me feel right old," he said. And he winked, as if we shared some sort of secret. "Still just a wisp of a thing, though."

Nana turned around then, in all her splendour. She was dressed in her trademark green rubber boots and khaki trousers, her hair tucked under the same mud-splattered hat she had worn so long I'm sure it was stuck like Velcro to her head.

She hugged me, the kind of hug that says don't go getting too mushy on me now, eh? Or, let's just get this over with. She smelled like always, too. It was a strange mixture of Lux soap and oatmeal—not bad smells one at a time but when you mix them together, just a bit sour. Nana Vinegar, like I said. Her chin hair was whiter than ever and longer too. She was a twin of one of those mountain goats in *National Geographic*, coincidentally her favourite magazine.

She grunted a thank you to Harv for chucking the bags up into the back of the pickup. We eased out onto the main road for about half a minute before turning onto a dirt road heading towards Boutillier's Point. When we rounded the bend by the barrel factory and

Ludlow's Lumberyard, the ocean spread out before us, dotted with islands. They looked like giant clusters of broccoli. It was a spectacular view. I had to gulp a bit and catch my breath when I spotted the house.

My father's house—the homestead, as he calls it—is built on a slab of land that juts out like a hitchhiker's thumb right into the Atlantic, at the entrance to Boulder Basin. A gingerbread house, some would call it. The trim along the eaves is all loops and dips and swirls like sugar frosting. Behind the house is a small, run-down barn, where Nana used to keep a pony, a pig and a few hens. Behind the barn is the hill. Just a hill too, although when I was little it seemed like a mountain. Walking up it took forever, and the grass was taller than I was. Things really do shrink as you get older. Still, it would be a good hill for training on, and the view from the top was, as Corporal Ray loved to say, a million-dollar view.

"What kind of get-up is that you got on?" Nana sniffed at me. That was it. Not "How was your trip, dear?" or "How are your folks?" First thing, she starts in, as if she's a fashion plate herself. But I was determined to get off on the right foot.

"Bell-bottoms, Nana."

"And what's with the dirt around your belly button?"

"It's a temporary tattoo. It's just a stencil, and it washes off."

"That's good, because you'll either be washing it off or making sure you wear something more decent that doesn't announce to the world you've got the ugliest belly button I've ever seen. It reminds me of a pollywog."

That's when it struck me that maybe she was about as thrilled with our summer arrangement as I was. I don't know what came over me, but I started to giggle. I couldn't stop.

"What's with you?" she snarled. She tried to scowl her fiercest witchy sour vinegar scowl.

I just kept laughing as she swung into the driveway. She braked so hard, if I hadn't had my seat belt fastened I would have gone clear through the windshield. She slammed out of the truck.

"Supper in an hour. You know where your room is. Get freshened up and don't be bringing the pollywog to the supper table."

She started up the steps to the veranda but stopped to rest halfway up, as if she had to catch her breath, something I'd never seen her do before. I got my duffel bag and followed.

Try as I might, as I showered that diesel fuel out of my hair, I never figured out how my belly button looked like a pollywog.

— SETTING THE RECORD STRAIGHT —

Part of me was terrified we'd have tongue of beef for supper. We had herring with new potatoes and fresh garden peas and sour cream and cucumbers. It was delicious. I did the dishes and cleaned up, then made a pot of tea. Nana went into the sunroom and smoked her corncob pipe. Tell me, what kind of grandmother smokes a pipe?

"Hot out the teapot first!" she shouted out. I did as I was told. Poured hot water into the pot, swished it around, poured it away, put the Red Rose tea bags in, then filled the pot with water up to the brim. The bags bobbed to the surface like swimmers with bloated bellies floating on their backs around the pot.

"By the end of the summer, I'll have you brewing lots more interesting kinds!" she shouted out.

Well, whoopdy-doo. Such fun ahead.

When I took in the tea, the sun was going down and the sky was streaked with fingers of cloud, all fluorescent pinks and golds. The ocean held the reflection, as if the sky had tumbled into the waves. I had been missing a long-lost friend, I thought. The ocean, I mean, not my Nana.

We sat in silence. There was the taste of salt in the breeze that was blowing in through the window. Yep. This place, this smell, that going-on-and-out-forever ocean gave me as much and maybe even more of a feeling of home than the one I'd just left. That was my last thought before I feel asleep that night.

I dreamt of snow. It was a dream of last winter, the day the baby died. My dream was like an Etch A Sketch drawing. I kept erasing the dream as I dreamt it. Then I woke up and remembered what really happened and that I couldn't erase it. I sat up in the dark and wished I could scrub the truth away and keep the dream I wanted.

I had to go to the bathroom. Too much information? No big deal, you think? Maybe if I were home. But I wasn't.

There were two things about going to the bathroom at the witch's house in the middle of the night that terrified me. First off, there were the moths. Big fat-bodied moths with bulgy eyes that came in through the window screen, swivelled around the light and then glued themselves to the baseboards for a good night's sleep. When you sat on the toilet seat they attacked your toes. For real. My grandmother said that was nothing but foolishness. She said this after I screamed myself silly in the middle of the night at age five.

Once, I worked up enough nerve and killed one. It crunched as if it had bones and splattered yellow guck. After that, killing was not an option. I learned to always wear socks and do my business fast.

As if the moths weren't bad enough, in order to go to the bathroom in the dead of night, in the darkest dark, I had to go past the Witch's Closet. Ever since I could remember, my grandmother had a padlock on this door. I even heard my mother ask my father what the big deal was. "What on earth does she do in there, Ray? What is she so damned secretive about?"

"Oh, I think it's just her stamp collection," my father said once, "and photos and stuff she's saved over the years. I think she even has some of my dad's old Wilf Carter records in there. Wouldn't mind taking a peek myself." But Nana guarded it like she was secret service at the Royal Canadian Mounted Police herself.

But once I saw it *open*. A naked light bulb dangled from a long chain. The ceilings were very high and my grandmother very short. A red ribbon was attached to a smaller chain to switch the bulb on and off. Nana turned and saw me peeking in at her. She clicked the light off and hid what was in her hands.

"Do *not* go snooping! You might not like what you find!"

I ran off crying for my mother but never told her what happened until years later.

"I think it was a skeleton," I told her. "In her hands, I think she had bones, lots of bones, a *bunch* of bones."

"Oh, honey, it was probably a dream or your O.I. going wonky. Besides," she said with a little laugh, "everyone's got skeletons in their closet, get it?"

Even though my mother tried to joke her way out of it, she didn't ever convince me. There *was* something spooky about that closet. And I know what I saw.

Besides, why did my mother always whistle really loud and walk super fast every time she passed the closet herself? It gave her the heebie-jeebies too. I know it did.

I scared myself more just lying there thinking on it. But I really had to go. What else to do? I *mustered* up my courage. How do you muster? I used to wonder when I heard folks say that. When I was really little I pictured myself covered with invisible mustard that kept away all bad things. Things that you didn't want to ketch up with you. Ha ha.

I confess that at the ripe old age of twelve the game still worked wonders. I sprinted safely to the bathroom. Whistling. There were only five moths and they slept the whole time!

On my way back, I tiptoed past the Witch's Closet. The door rattled. Maybe it was unlocked. I could go in. If I wanted.

If I dared.

I reached out. The knob was as cold as metal in winter. I turned it. The door didn't even budge.

I sprinted back to my room. Nana mumbled in her sleep. I held my breath. She snored.

By then I was wide-awake as a Saturday morning. I started reading. It worked, finally, but it was sunrise when I fell back to sleep. Nana shouted up not long after that.

"Get up—get cracking!" She had the same squawking voice as the gulls circling the basin and shrieking the day to life outside my bedroom window. You should have heard her down there, clomping across the kitchen floor, rattling the drawers on purpose. It's amazing how one little old lady could make such a racket. The radio was up full blast and she was whistling away, off key. I think it was "I've Been Working on the Railroad" or some other cheery working or wake-up song. She'd already have written out a list of chores longer than her arm for me because "idle hands come to no good" or however it went.

"Early to bed, early to rise, the early bird gets the worm," she shouted up just then.

"Eat your oatmeal by yourself and may your tongue stick to the roof of your mouth for all I care," I muttered. I gagged at the very smell of her porridge.

Besides, I had a plan. I would take an hour for running first thing every day. That way, I could avoid sitting across the table from her and wouldn't have to listen to her dentures snap when she chewed.

I got dressed beneath the covers. Not only was I afraid she'd burst into my room like a tornado at any moment, but it was so cold it was polar. Even by midsummer, this house would be damp and clammy and she'd still be poking wood in the stove to take the chill out like she was doing now. Much as I love the place, it's always too cold and smells like the dust of potatoes kept too long in the storage cellar.

"Going out for my run, Nana!" I whooped out over the din. I was flying down those stairs. I knew if nothing else, I had a bit of speed going for me.

"Get back here. Minn! Cinnamon Elizabeth Hotchkiss! What do—?"

"Training, Nan, Dad must have told you."

She was on the veranda then watching me stretch. "Going to the Olympics now, are you?" she huffed.

"Who knows?"

"Well, ambition's good if you got talent to go with it and even talent's not gonna do you a lick of good unless you got some breakfast in your belly first."

"I've got my sports drink."

"It's blue."

"So?"

"You can't tell me that blue juice first thing in the morning is good for you. Gut rot. That's what that is, gut rot. Eating anything blue is not natural."

"What about blueberries?"

"Don't you sass me!"

"See you in an hour!"

"Get back here! There'll be no breakfast for you. I'm not running a restaurant here this summer . . . and furthermore . . . ah, Chicoutimi!"

As I rounded the bend, I heard the door slam. Slam dunk for me, I thought. She had to know from the start I didn't need a babysitter or someone telling me what to do.

— BEACHCOMBING —

The running that morning wasn't easy. Maybe it was all the energy I'd just wasted, maybe it was the dirt road, and maybe I should have had at least an orange. Ten minutes into my run, for crying out loud, for no reason at all, I started crying out loud. I don't mean crying just a little, I mean bawling like a lunatic. I couldn't seem to stop, either the running or the crying, and I don't know what was running faster, my nose or me.

I slowed down a little, though, when I saw a black limousine snaking through the poplar trees up ahead on Poplar Hill. My heart did a cartwheel in my chest.

Carolina was right! It had been a rumour for years, but maybe just maybe Hardly Whynot did have a summer home here. Who else in Boulder Basin would be driving a limousine? It turned out of Poplar Lane and headed towards me. I could make out the silhouette of a chauffeur through the windshield. Hat, sunglasses. The real thing.

Any minute now, it would drive up alongside of me. The window of the limo would slide open silently. Mr. Whynot himself would lean out, saying, "Aye, mate, out for a run, are we?" I knew what he looked like and how he talked because my mother made me watch the old movies so many times. Then I would tell him that my mother was his biggest fan ever and he was the only man she ever loved besides my dad Corporal Ray and how her lifelong wish was to get his autograph. Could I please have one for her? He would say yes. And my mother would be grateful she had one daughter at least.

But not like this. I couldn't meet someone that famous and British and make an impression looking like this! Not even for my mother. I knew my eyes were swollen from my yanging and my nose all crusty. No. Proper introductions are important in our house. I crossed the road.

I scrambled over the boulders lining the shore and started leaping from one rock to another towards the ocean. Jack be nimble, Minn be quick! I sang to myself. It was a dangerous thing to do, not because of the ocean— the tide was out—but it would be all too easy to sprain my ankle. That would be the end of my running for the summer, not to mention the only means of escape from my grandmother. I slowed down to smaller hops.

As the limo passed, I peeked back up. The chauffeur gave me a thumbs-up. His sunglasses were the ski goggle models. He was probably a bodyguard as well and was checking me out, making sure I wasn't a sniper in disguise. He looked long enough to get a physical description. Subject: *Pre-teen girl. Hair: honeyblondebrown. Eyes: bluegray-green. Height: short. Wgt.: featherweight. Distinguishing feature: freckles unevenly distributed across bridge of nose. Status: newcomer. Potential stalker.*

Cool as a cucumber, or so I hoped, I nodded. It was a nod that said: "To me you are just another limo and I am not suspicious about your boss. I am not impressed by your fancy car and I am not Nancy Drew or Trixie Belden, girl detective." But that's exactly how I felt.

The limo sped on down the road, leaving a plume of dust behind it.

At the water's edge, I walked on for a while, stopping now and then to bend down and snap the seaweed pods. The clumps of dried-out seaweed by the road were the colour of ashes. Cheerleaders' pompoms. But these clustered ones, the fresh ones, were the colour of dry mustard and made a snapping sound until they gave a little wheeze and oozed out a spit of water. The other kind of seaweed reminded me of lasagna: long ribbons of seaweed littered across the sand, as if the mermaids had had some wild party and the streamers were left over next day for someone to come and pick up.

You can't move anything by the ocean's edge without noticing how everything is connected. The barnacles on the rocks, the tiny pool of water with crabs scuttling for safety. Then there's the spiders, always looking like they are on some sort of mission. Spiders with a plan. *Must get to school, must get to market, must get to work and spin my web.*

A few feet away from where the bank of rocks ended was a strip of beach. The sand was a fudgy brown and polka-dotted with clam holes. Just last summer we were in about this same spot, digging clams for supper. Corporal Ray loved to pretend he was the clam in each hole. In a squeaky voice like some cartoon character he'd start in: *Don't dig here, please spare my life. Go next door— the meat is much more tender next door. Oh, thank you, kind sir, now I'm happy as a clam, ha ha ha.* By the time we had a bucket full and went home to boil them and dip them in butter, I could barely eat them for the guilt of taking their lives. But I had learned you eat what's put in front of you at Nana's. I laughed at the thought of my father and his foolishness. Then I had a flash: a picture of him and my mother holding hands in the sunset. They could have been the cover of one of Carolina's romance novels, I thought as I walked back towards Nana's. So I erased the picture from my mind with a shake of my head, as if I had water in my ear. What was wrong with me? I had that sad throat again. I started beachcombing as if I was searching for gold.

— DISCOVERY —

I found a sand dollar, a starfish and a sea urchin and stuffed them in the pocket of my sweatshirt. Then I settled myself on a large, flat rock. The sun dried my face. The waves sloshed into shore in time with my breathing and the beating of my heart. I don't know how long I sat there, but too soon the tide was coming back in—my signal to head back up the road.

In front of Nana's house, the rocks were smaller and clacked together beneath my feet like marbles in a pouch. This gave me an idea. Perhaps I should bring her a peace offering. I started to look for heart-shaped rocks. I'd been collecting them for years. And so had Nana. It was the only thing you might say we had in common. All I ever found were crooked hearts, but it seemed to me that if I looked long enough, some day I might just find that perfect heart-shaped rock. Yes, I might even give it to the witch. Or not.

A person's eyes could get buggy from looking so long at the ground.

Just as I was about to give up, an odd-shaped shell caught my eye. I figured some creature lived in it, judging from the shape it was in. Maybe the gulls ate the inside and bashed it on the rocks the way they did with mussels. It was the size of a tennis ball, I'd say, but more oval than round. I poked it with a stick at first, to make sure some spider with shark teeth wouldn't attack. I turned it over. It was hard to believe that the scream I heard was my own.

It was a tiny, perfect human skull.

∾ Departures ∾

The trip to Liverpool by train was grim. Mum cried as we
pulled out of the station. Dad tried to lighten things but
didn't have much luck. I stared out at the countryside passing
by until Dad gave up his cheery act and fell asleep. The only
thing louder than his snoring was the train itself. The clickety-
clack and screaming engines, the whistle blowing every time it
slowed down and chugged through another village.

Thomas looked like someone dreaming while awake. Yes,
he was with us! I was over the moon. But he sure wasn't
happy about it. Even I couldn't get Rebecca's face out of my
mind. When they rushed up to the train and Thomas
jumped on at the last second, her eyes were puffy from her
sobbing. And she looked at me as if I'd committed a mur-
der. She may as well have said if it weren't for you my heart
would not be breaking. I felt a pang—a little teeny pang—
of guilt. Very teeny. After all, he was *my* brother before he
was her beau.

But so much for the happy travels everyone had wished us. I tried to read, but the motion of the train turned my belly inside out. The smell of coal? Sickening! To make matters worse it started to rain. Since money was tight, we were riding in an open coach. We were getting wet.

Dad woke up and tried to cover us with a blanket and looked up into the night sky.

"Thank the good Lord for relatives," he said. "I trust your cousin Libby will have a good meal and a dry bed for us." Then he shouted and pointed. "Ahead, boys, Liverpool's just ahead."

Thomas and I stood up and strained over the tops of folks' heads to get a look. There were pinpricks of fire in the distance.

"Gas lamps!" said Thomas.

I'd never seen anything like it. "It's as if all the stars in the Milky Way have fallen from the sky!" I said.

"Liverpool today—tomorrow the world!" Dad clapped his hands together. "It'll be good to taste that ocean air." He kissed the top of Tom's head. "You'll see, son. All your life's before you still."

Thomas nodded and gave half a grin. For one second, his eyes danced. I beamed at him.

He narrowed his eyes and scowled.

❧ Farewells ❧

"Go do your business, John, it'll be the last comfortable dump you have for weeks."

"Thomas, really!" said Mum, blushing in front of her cousin. Thomas nudged me when she went round the back, though. First chance the water closet was vacant.

Libby's husband, Harold, navigated the carriage through the narrow, crowded streets of the city to the dockyard. It was a grey day. The city was wrapped in fog thicker than a woollen blanket. Libby explained it was more than fog.

"It's the poison in the air from all the industry. It'll be worse where you're going to."

Thomas shot her a withering look. "Thanks for your kindly words of encouragement," he muttered to me.

When we reached the dockyard we were sucked into the whirlwind of energy. The ground beneath us vibrated.

"John, over here! Take a look at that, would you?" Thomas pulled my arm. He was pointing to a ship.

"That's ours?"

He nodded.

"Are you sure?" I choked out. I was looking up and up and up. I was getting dizzier by the second.

"What's the matter, little brother, getting scared?"

"Not likely!" I said, but kept hold of his coattails.

The men working on that giant, whale-shaped boat beetled to and fro, carrying crates on their backs and pushing them into holes darker than the mouths of underground caves. The stench in the air was overpowering—sweat and rotting fish and salt and more coal mingled together.

I retched—and vomited my breakfast. On Tom's shoe.

"John! Disgusting! Here," he said. He wiped my face with a brisk rub of his handkerchief. "Quick now, before Mum sees and makes a big fuss. You'll be fine. Just too much excitement. Breathe."

"I'd rather not. That's the problem."

"Then plug your nose. Like this. Just scrunch it up and then breathe through your mouth." His voice changed as he showed me. I did as I was told. It worked.

Single file, holding on to each other, we wove our way through the crowd. Finally, we reached a man in uniform at the head of a long queue of people. He frowned as he shuffled through the handful of papers and tickets Dad handed over. He looked at the crate and cradle, shook his head. I watched Dad slip some money into the man's palm. He waved us forward.

Thomas jabbed me in the ribs. "Told you about them. Was I right or what?" I followed his finger.

At the stern of the ship, on a thick cable of rope leading up to another one of those dark holes, was a rat as big as a beagle. It crawled up a twist of rope and into the belly of the ship. We both shivered. Rats spread the plague that claimed our grandparents' lives. Now that was a story that haunted us even more than legends of the Black Knight.

"It's time," said Dad. He was pale beneath his usual browned face. Mum sobbed into Libby's shoulder and Libby was bawling too.

"For God's sake, Mare," Dad said as we walked up the gangplank to the main deck, "I didn't think you even liked the woman."

"It's not Libby I'm crying for, it's England," she sniffled.

Dad came to a dead halt. Thomas and I bumped into them.

"We can turn around right now, Mary Hindley. It's not too late. They'll give me my job back in a second at the mill—you know that. Are you sure this is what you want?"

I held my breath.

Mum reached up and passed her hand across Dad's forehead like she was feeling for a fever. "You are the kindest man alive, Paddy. I thank you for asking that question."

Thomas rolled his eyes.

"Move along, mates." The voice behind us was friendly but impatient.

Goodbyes are many things all mixed up together, I thought as we took our place on deck.

The ship's horn sounded. Throngs of people waved and a cheer went up from those left behind. Libby was now just a little dot of red and black, like a ladybug, I thought as she got smaller and smaller and smaller.

The grinding and moaning of the ship was deafening. We headed with purpose for open waters. Thomas's hand covered mine. At first I thought it was some sort of accident. But no.

"Wave, John Hindley, wave goodbye to the shores of our homeland, and I'll wave goodbye to my heart."

"Oh brother!" Oh lovesick brother.

I was all ready to pretend to blow kisses back to Rebecca, but Thomas moved his hand just then. He placed a protective arm around my shoulder.

I held my teasing back and we stood on deck a very long time, as did most folks, stood there until the last speck of land turned a pale grey and seemed to melt finally, blurring into the line between the sky and the sea. England disappeared as easily as a cloud rubbed out by wind.

— THE BONE CLOSET —

"'Bout time," Nana snapped from behind the door, as if she'd been lying in wait for me the whole time. She had a purple plastic flyswatter in her hand. I half expected her to start swatting me in the back of the legs with it when I brushed past her to go upstairs. I wanted to wash the skull and get a better look at it.

"Suppose you're hungry now. Well, we better get something straight right off about meals—"

"What?" I said, trying to keep my voice as neutral as I could.

"You look like you've seen a ghost or something," she said.

"I did," I said, then pulled the skull out from under my shirt and thrust it in her face. I was hoping to freak her out. She barely blinked. Then she turned so fast she squeaked. I'm certain I could smell rubber burning from her boots.

"Bring it into the kitchen first," she said. "Then I'll put it with the others."

The others?

I followed her into the kitchen.

"Just put it on the table," she ordered.

She cleared a spot by shoving aside what looked to me like my breakfast. I suppose it would have been my punishment for running off. She would have made me eat a bowl full of cold porridge.

She filled the sink up with warm sudsy water and then motioned to me to bring it over.

"It's yours. You have to clean it." She handed me an old toothbrush. "Be gentle."

I scrubbed at least ten minutes. As the dirt dislodged from the cavities and pockmarks, the skull became more recognizably human.

"Okay, that'll do," she said and held out a terrycloth towel. I watched as she dried every nook and cranny, and even used a Q-tip on the smaller spaces she couldn't get at with the twisted corner of the towel. She handed the skull back to me. But it was the strangest thing. It no longer felt like a skull. It felt like a head. It was warmer for one thing. It gave me the heebie-jeebies.

Nana clasped the key that hung from a rope around her neck and pulled it over her head. Or tried to. She was wearing an oversized man's plaid shirt and the key got tangled up in her collar. After tugging for a bit, she finally croaked from beneath the folds of the shirt, "Help me with this, would ya?"

Rather trusting, I thought, letting me help her with a rope around her neck.

When she had the key in her hand and her shirt back in place, she pointed to the skull and then upstairs. With the skull in my hands—like a dead weight, which it was—I followed.

She cackled. "I call this the bone closet."

Just as I feared and always suspected. There *was* something secret and deadly behind that locked door. Great, I was thinking, she's a vampire witch and I'm in the middle of a horror movie.

But at first, it was nothing spectacular. A small storage room. I smelled mothballs and cedar and stifled a sneeze. There were books and boxes everywhere. Herbs hung upside down in bunches. She reached behind a neat stack of shoeboxes and chocolate boxes and scooped up bundles of dirty old tea towels. Cradling them in her arms as if she was carrying a baby, she placed the five bundles on a steamer trunk.

"Unwrap them," she instructed. The creepy feeling slithered into my belly again.

"No," I whispered.

She laughed. "They won't bite."

"I'm telling Dad," I said.

"What?"

"That you're scaring me."

"You've got yourself worked up, is all," she said and laughed again. "Your imagination's far worse than the truth. Unwrap them."

So I did.

I let a yelp out of me that travelled to Katmandu and back. Sure enough, there were more bones and partial skulls.

"Calm down," the witch was snorting. Laughing! "Don't look so terrified. It's not like I ever killed anyone!"

I had to plug my nose for fear of upchucking right there on the floor. I started to back out of the closet.

"No you don't, get back here. It's not pleasant but it's a fact. I figure this here was a man, this one a woman, this child, maybe four, five years old. You found a baby this morning. See?"

She put her glasses on and rummaged through a wicker basket. From a rat's nest of trinkets she produced a measuring tape and proceeded to measure the baby's skull.

"Not more than two months old, I'd say. God bless her little soul."

"Nana, what's going on?" The room was starting to wobble in front my eyes, like heat rising from hot pavement in summer.

"Out!" she hissed. She didn't have to tell me twice.

She locked the door behind her. "Put on some boots. I've got someplace to take you."

"I didn't bring any."

"There's an extra pair of rubbers by the door."

She grabbed the keys to her truck. I didn't even have time to untie my sneakers, just threw them off and stepped into boots miles too big for me. I clomped after her as fast as I could. She was already in the truck with the motor gunning by the time I caught up with her.

— GRAVE SIGHTS —

"It's only five minutes from here."

"What's five minutes from here? Where are you taking me?" She had a wild-eyed look about her. Crazy, I kept thinking, my whole family is bonkers now.

"You'll see when we get there."

She sped like a demon down the main highway, then turned onto a dirt road I'd never been on before. It was narrow and cut through dense forest of fir and pine. We were in the middle of nowhere. I hadn't seen a house for at least a mile. Nana honked suddenly.

It was a squirrel. The truck hit the soft dirt on the shoulder of the road and fishtailed until she finally got control. And she just kept on going!

"Nana!" I screamed.

"Relax," she said, "I'm a very good driver." Compared to who? I wondered.

After a few more hair-raising twists and turns, she

parked. We got out of the truck and she looked around, almost as if she was sniffing for danger.

"Hold still," she said. I turned in time to get showered with bug spray. She just missed my eyes.

"The no-see-ums are buggers this time of year. They get me every time." She doused herself with the musky stuff, dabbing it behind her ears as if it were perfume from Paris. From the cab of the truck, she pulled out a stick and some bells.

"Never seen a bear in these here woods, and never want to neither. Just in case, though, this'll scare them off." I think she thought it was a good joke. I didn't laugh.

She crossed the road and clambered down into the ditch, motioning to me to follow with an impatient wave of her arm. I squished after her, darn near sinking in mud the colour and thickness of tar. I had to fight my way through a grove of cattails, most of them taller than I was. Nana was breathing heavily by this time, but then so was I.

"Shh!" she hissed, looking behind me. I slowly turned. It wasn't a skeleton or a bear, but a doe, just a few steps away. She noticed us, and with a flick of tail showing the white patch around its bottom like a thong bikini, she was gone.

"This way," said Nana. An overgrown trail led deeper into the forest. "Careful of the branches," she said. "One snap in the eye and you'll be blind for the rest of your life."

I followed at a safe distance as they whipped back. She was ploughing through like some dog on the scent of a rabbit. The wild blackberry bushes and thistles on either side of the trail attacked my ankle bones. Finally, we made it to some sort of a clearing.

Panting, she trudged up a small knoll in the centre of the clearing. I joined her, almost blown over by the force of the wind, gasping at what I saw. It was a view of the ocean even more spectacular than from the hill behind her house. Stretching out as far as I could see was nothing but ocean. It was a wild and thrashing sea, the roar of the waves like thunder beneath our feet.

"Over here," she shouted. Barely visible for the alders and scrub brush around it was a cemetery. The tombstones were lopsided, crooked teeth in a dinosaur's jaw. She pointed to a tall monument, a giant cement pencil pointing to the sky. "Looks like a miniature of the Washington Monument, doesn't it?" she wheezed.

"I couldn't say," I said, "seeing as I've never seen the Washington Monument." I was hot and bruised and frustrated and now wet by the spray from waves hitting the rocks below. I couldn't look down without getting dizzy.

"Well, it does. Read what it says," she ordered.

There was a rectangular plaque, tarnished from age, about halfway up the base of the stone. I read it out loud.

"'This spot marks the burial of some 544 souls lost at sea in the marine disaster of the SS *Atlantic* on April 1, 1873. May they rest in the waters of eternal life.'"

"Five hundred and fo—" I was astonished.

"Everyone knows about the *Titanic*," Nana said quietly. "They write books about it, make movies and spend millions looking for it. That's fine, it should be remembered. But this shipwreck was the largest wreck before the *Titanic*. This one is all but forgotten. Nearly everyone in Boulder Basin and Terns Bay helped in the rescue that night." She pointed just down the coast aways. "See that hump of rock out there, like a whale's back?"

I nodded. It was only visible every few moments, as waves crashed around it.

"That's where she hit. Not even eight hundred feet from Elbow Island beyond. Some made it to the island. Some washed up on its shore. Some say if you step on that island to this day you'll hear the screams and dying words of those who didn't make it. Those bones you found, they're from here, this gravesite where those folks got buried. Time and the sea are eroding the earth. These poor buggers are drowning all over again."

"You mean the bones from here make it all the way to your house?"

"All up and down this coast these past few years. Before that, people around here collected enough treasures and pieces of ship in their houses to set up a small museum. Which is exactly what I'd like to see someday. Anyhow, the erosion of the grave itself is a tragedy. I've been stashing the bones for a few years now, hoping I could get some action."

"Action for what?"

"To restore this gravesite, first off. Thought we could fix up the shoreline here, bulldoze some earth back in and build up the embankment to keep who's left buried safe. I started off writing a few letters. I went to some town council meetings."

"What happened?"

"They told me it would cost too much—and the municipality doesn't have that much money. Bullcrap. They have enough for their new yacht club and the cobblestone patio where all I can tell is just for the tourists and come from aways to go get drunk on Friday nights. I even wrote the government. Haven't heard a word."

"But what's this got to do with you keeping a closet full of bones?"

"When I have enough I'm going to just march into Riley Tucker's office—he's our member of Parliament —and dump them on his desk."

"Nana, you wouldn't!"

"Yes, I would, then demand somebody save the grave. These folks were someone's families. Everyone deserves a proper burial." Her voice was barely a whisper. But fierce as the sea. A loud kathump of wave crashed just underneath us. "Besides, it's just not good having lost souls floating around the area. Strange things start happening."

"You mean ghosts?" I couldn't believe I was hearing this from No-Nonsense herself.

"No. I mean spirits—like I said. The dead should not be disturbed. It's bad enough they hang around out there on Elbow Island. We don't want them here on shore."

"Nana, let's go back."

"All right. If you're interested, I've got a heap of stuff at the house for you to look through. Magazine articles and clippings, some letters, in those boxes in the bone closet." She was almost smiling.

"Nah. I've got enough to do with my training." A flicker of something passed over her face. Disappointment? Hurt?

"Fine, I figured you'd be too chicken anyhow." Her voice was pulled tight and sharp as barbed wire.

"I'm not afraid, Nana! I could handle it. I'm just not interested." This was a bald-faced lie. She already had me hooked. I just wouldn't give her the satisfaction. It was that old harbour of hate, I suppose.

"Someday you'll realize it's better to be more curious than afraid."

We drove back home in a silence as thick as the fog that was rolling in.

— UNDERCOVER RESEARCH —

It was well after supper when I ran my laps, sprints up and down that hill ten times. The feathery light of dusk fanned out into complete darkness. Tar Black. Black Raven. Darkest Black. Black Widow. Sorrow's Black.

On the last lap I stopped at the top and looked long and hard out at that ocean. It was a calm night. The water was still but looked cold and oily, as if lying in wait to swallow a shipload of people. I could make out the faint shape of Elbow Island. Nana's words of it being haunted by spirits revved up my O.I. It was in full spooky mode. I searched the sky, hoping for the comfort my father believed could be found there. The moon was a lopsided canoe hanging in the sky. The clouds were phantoms peering down at me from beyond the beyond. There wasn't so much as a star for comfort. I ran fast as I could back to the house.

Nana was watching *Jeopardy*, one of her favourites. When I went to get a drink of water, I noticed she'd left the key to the bone closet on the table. I slipped it in my pocket.

"Who is Marco Polo?" I shouted out before she could on my way through the TV room. She grunted her displeasure.

"Night, Nana, I'm going to have a shower and then get into bed."

"Night what is helium?" she said all in one breath. She's in love with Alex Trebek. "He was born in Canada, you know," she says every time the theme song starts playing. Repetition is another irritating habit of hers. This was also on my list of reasons I did not love her like a normal grandchild.

After I got in bed, I set my watch alarm. It was my only chance to find out more without her knowing.

It went off at exactly 4:22.

I crept along the hall. Every step creaked.

"One thousand one, one thousand two . . ." I counted to fifteen between each step. It worked. The witch did not wake up. The lock was stubborn, though, and I inched the door open, cringing with every squeak. Nana rolled over, muttering in her sleep. Finally I made it in.

Utter blackness. I had to feel my way along the wall.

Something—a wisp of hair, maybe—brushed my forehead. I smothered a scream. It was just the frayed end of the ribbon on the chain. I yanked the light on. I picked out a stack of chocolate boxes and shoeboxes.

Then I reached into the hiding place. My hand touched one of the bundles of bones. I swear every hair on my head stood up like I'd just rubbed my scalp with a balloon. But I felt around until I found the baby's skull. It was my find, after all.

I turned off the light and scampered back to my room.

I examined the skull. I tried imagining the face of the baby it belonged to. A girl or a boy? Dimples? Brown eyes or blue?

I tucked it underneath my pillow. Then I arranged the boxes out on my quilt. I opened the first box and glanced through the contents. I began to read. And then I read and read. Oh, did I read.

The accounts of the disaster were gruesome. Article after article and photocopies of old newspapers from places as far away as New York were covered in plastic.

DREADFUL WRECK!
— THE LOSS OF THE S.S. ATLANTIC —
544 Lives LOST!
WHEN, HOW AND WHERE THE WRECK TOOK PLACE.
SCENES ON SHORE, ON BOARD AND IN THE WATER

I read enough to figure out the obvious—the shipwreck was world news at the time. Nowadays, it would be all over CNN. And it was beyond disaster.

-Minute by Minute-

"I suppose it is not necessary," said one of the crew, "to give you the minute particulars of how EACH LIFE was lost. Every succeeding minute waves washed off one, two, three; sometimes six, then a dozen were SWEPT AWAY and went out side by side into the valley of death. There is no language that can describe the feelings of a man holding on for DEAR LIFE to a bit of rigging and watching his friends and companions struggling, clutching, SINKING, DYING. The weakest of course went first . . . "

The words made the pictures clear enough for me. Sifting through the newsprint was like putting together the pieces of a novel with the chapters out of order.

My grandmother, in her own handwriting, had compiled passenger lists: Cabin Passengers, Steerage Passengers, Crew and Officers, Firemen/Trimmers, Storekeepers, Stewards. Name after name after name, and sometimes their ages.

I skimmed through them at first. The A's, the B's, the C's. By the time I got to the D's, I began to whisper their names. When I got to the H's—H as in Hotchkiss—I was saying them out loud.

"Michael Higgins (32).

"W. P. Hill (22).

"Patrick Hindley (40).

"Mary Hindley (38).

"Thomas Hindley (15).

"John Hindley (12).

"John Hoadley (26).

"G. T. M. Hoadley (2).

"Isabella Hoadley (infant).

"Margaret Hoadley (23).

"William Hogan . . ."

At that point, my eyes felt as if they were bleeding. I realized I was crying. Whole entire families. *Baby Isabella.* A boy *my age.* His older brother, just fifteen. *Thomas.* It was my father's middle name.

I didn't know I could feel so much for folks I never knew. Isabella never got a chance, I thought. *Like Pippa.*

John—Did he live or die? Was he one of the weakest?

"And who were you, Thomas?" I asked out loud. "A fine young man? Did you live or die? Were you handsome? Were you strong enough to swim to shore?" I pictured him for a second, a smiling, sandy-haired teenager. Strong.

My grandmother had two other lists, Passengers Lost and Passengers Saved. I couldn't bring myself to read them. I just couldn't. I closed that box and pulled a black chocolate box onto my lap. It was criss-crossed with red elastic bands. It looked like a miniature coffin. I just sat there, holding it on my lap for a few minutes.

I was afraid that if I opened it, I would find more bones.

— YIKES! —

Nana's bedsprings squeaked. She was getting up! I grabbed my mess of articles, stuffed them back into their boxes, did a running tip-toe dash to the bone closet, crammed everything back in, closed the door, replaced the key, sprinted back and dove beneath my covers. Phew! She was still in her room, coughing and piddling and making other noises so loud, no way could she have heard me.

I tucked the baby's skull beneath my other pillow. I tossed and turned. Finally, I drifted off. I wouldn't call it sleep exactly. And as for peaceful?

The reading fuelled my O.I. Not the first time, I have to admit, and the reason I have the only parents in the world who do not encourage bedtime reading. *Alice in Wonderland* gave me night horrors. So did the wicked witch in the Disney version of *Sleeping Beauty*. I was only allowed peaceful bedtime stories.

The nightmare started out pretty cozy. I was in a small house with Dory and Corporal Ray. We were going on a trip. Corporal Ray was yodelling up a storm. Next thing I knew we were on the deck of a ship. A sinking ship. And I was sliding off. I watched my mother and father swallowed by a wave. I went underwater and grabbed a piece of wood. I came up sputtering for air, rocking on top of the waves. I was cold. Bone cold.

I woke up shivering. I'd seen the movie *Titanic* one too many times. It was one of Carolina's favourites and she was crazy over Leonardo DiCaprio. She shared my mother's worship of celebrities. I thought instead of the Swiss Family Robinson. I'd float to an island and survive like they did. This made me think of snakes, however. So I closed my eyes and tried to think happy thoughts. My mother encouraged me to do this when I was overly agitated, as she put it.

A picture of Gavin filled the screen inside my head. Not happy thoughts exactly, and not very calming either. My heart popped three wheelies in a row.

— RIGBYISMS —

Next morning, all thoughts of shipwrecks and Gavin were swept away like bits of dirt under a carpet.

A letter from Coach Rigby arrived. It was my daily training schedule for the next five weeks along with his special brand of coaching from the sidelines.

Dear Twinkletoes:

Thought I'd give you a day or two off before I hit you with THE PROGRAM. It's no doubt going to be tough to muster up the self-discipline that training by yourself requires. So along with the schedule, I've included some words of advice and creative visualization exercises. Remember, the mental aspect of training is what sometimes makes the difference between winners and losers. Attitude! The right attitude can get you over the hurdles ahead—no pun intended—Ha! Ha! So, I know you can do it! Paste my Rigbyism of the

*week on your mirror or the foot of your bed. Before you
get up in the morning and last thing at night I'd like
you to faithfully do these exercises like I know you will
tackle the rest of your physical regimen.*

*I'll call in a week or so. I've enclosed a training
diary for your convenience.*

                                        Coach Rigby

My first week's training schedule looked fair enough.
It was in a small black three-ring binder, and every day I
had to fill out what I did, when, what the weather was
like and what I felt like after I'd done it. On a scale of
one to ten.

His Rigbyism was another matter.

*Like the postal worker who delivers the mail through
rain snow sleet or hail, so must the committed athlete
endure all kinds of weather conditions—of climate and
mind—your internal weather system, in order to
deliver a most important message to yourself: I AM A
WINNER! Picture yourself bursting through the finish line, coming first, the crowd cheering you to victory.
See it, hear it, smell it, taste it, feel it. Rain or shine—
get out there and train for the win!*

I tried. I really tried. But when I closed my eyes all I
saw was a movie of disaster. There I was, all dressed up

like a letter carrier, in the baggiest uniform you ever saw, staggering up the track in lane number five. Oh, I was trying my best, but the mail bag bumped against my knees, tangled me up and felt like a hunk of cement chained to my neck. On top of that, I was running in a blizzard. With every in breath, I swallowed snow. By the time I wobbled to the finish line, it was dark and everybody had gone home, but I still raised my arms in a victory salute and shouted: "I'm a sinner! I mean a whiner! No—a winner—that's it!" Fade to black.

Poor Coach Rigby. He had no idea what sort of seeds he planted in my overactive imagination.

There was no sign of Nana at breakfast. She did leave me a note.

Gone to a U-pick up the road for strawberries. Eat.
P.S. Snooping is not polite.

Great. What did that mean? I wasn't tempted to open up that bone closet. The key was gone, and truthfully, even in the light of day, images of what I'd read the night before gave me a pain in my heart. So I studied my morning's routine, laced up my sneakers and headed out.

As I approached the hill near Poplar Grove, I spotted the limousine. I was a bit sweaty, but my nose was clean. I decided to face the car head on. Maybe there'd be a chance to see in the smoked-glass window. If it was some little old lady, I could forget about the foolishness of Hardly being around these parts.

The chauffeur bodyguard saluted to me. He slowed down. I kept running on my side of the road but he stopped in front of me. He left the car idling, got out, folded his arms, leaned against the door and waited for me to reach him.

My entire Mountie-daughter training told me to keep on going. He was, after all, a stranger. Limousine or no limousine, he could still be a pervert, a murderer, a thief or a kidnapper. Not that he would get much money from my folks seeing as they weren't exactly rolling in dough.

I stopped and eyed him up and down.

"You lost or something?" I shouted over.

"I've got a question for you."

"Yeah?" I was doing my tough voice. Carolina taught me that voice. It went with the don't-mess-with-me look. I struck my boxer's stance and clenched my fists by my side. Corporal Ray, despite my mother's protests, had insisted on basic boxing lessons. When I was eight. My left hook wasn't bad.

"How old are you?"

"Who wants to know?"

"I do."

"Who are you?"

"Long story."

"Why do you want to know my age?" I sniffed and started to run on the spot.

"Are you Ida Hennigar's granddaughter?"

"I don't talk to strangers."

He laughed. "You already are," he said with a grin wider than a pumpkin's. He certainly seemed friendly enough. Then again, that's how they lure their victims, said a warning voice inside my head.

If only he'd take off those sunglasses. They made him look sinister. Pervert or? Maybe he was Mafia or a Hells Angel, leader of a drug ring. Lots of drugs were smuggled in along the coast. Just last summer Corporal Ray had pored over the newspapers when we were here. Not twenty miles away from Boulder Basin there was a big drug bust.

"A little too close to home for comfort," he said to my mother and grandmother. "Things weren't like that when I was a kid."

"For heaven's sake," said Nana. "It's always been like that! Haven't I told you about your great-uncle Bob Countaway? Made a fortune as a rum-runner during Prohibition. Yes, everyone knew too, but even the police made the odd visit now and then to old Gordie, the boot-legger your uncle Bob kept well supplied. Yes. So now it's drugs, and if you ask my opinion alcohol's just as danger-ous in the hands of those who've got the sickness."

My father nodded at her with a grin.

"Did you ever make a trip to old Gordie's yourself, Ma?"

"Stop your foolishness. You know my blueberry wine's about the strongest thing I've ever poured down my gullet. Even then, only on special occasions, you know that."

My father winked at me and went back to the paper. All this came rushing back to me as I stood face to face almost—but not in grabbing distance of—the man who could be a drug smuggler. Yes, my O.I. was working just fine that morning. "Get your head out of the clouds," Corporal Ray always teased. *Used* to tease.

"The thing is," the chauffeur said, "I was wondering if I could take your picture?" He held up a camera.

Pervert! "What for?" I asked.

"The album."

Ohmygod. Had to be! He must be Hardly Whynot's personal photographer! I took off like a skittish colt.

I ran as far as Ludlow's Lumberyard and ducked behind an old shed and made my way to the shoreline. I was sweating and my nose was running again. I had no tissue.

Out at sea, a buoy clanged. Thoughts of the shipwreck surged up from where I thought I had tucked them safely away. The buoy clanged louder. And then I heard the voice.

— STRANGER STRANGERS —

"Looking for buried treasure?"

I spun around. The sun hit me full in the face. I shaded my eyes as he stepped forward, then cantered, graceful as a sure-footed horse, over those rocks, the muscles in his legs rippling. That's the part of him I saw first. Those strong legs. I stepped back a bit and stumbled.

"Whoa!" he said and grabbed my arm. I pulled away and fell anyhow.

"Cnicus benedictus!"

"Excuse me?" He was laughing.

I scowled up at him, rubbing my elbow. The sun had left spots in front of me, big purplish circles that still hid his face.

"You think it's funny? I could have sprained my ankle."

"Sorry. Here—"

He held out his hand. I hesitated. He leaned forward. And then I saw his face. Well, not all of it at first because those eyes just cancelled out the rest of the details. They were a blue I'd never seen before—or since. A blue shot through with light dancing behind it. But not sky or ocean blue. Even my mother would be hard pressed to come up with a name for this sort of blue. Faded Denim? Not that it mattered, because whatever the colour they had the power to make me reach out my hand. To a total stranger. Corporal Ray's warnings were pushed far to the back of my mind. His grip was tight. And warm. With as much dignity as I could muster, I wobbled up.

I felt my nose running. I looked down at the ground and wiped my sleeve over my upper lip to catch any drippings. But I hoped I made it look as though I was just itchy.

"Thanks," I mumbled into my sleeve.

"What's that?"

"Thanks," I said again and looked up at him.

"You're welcome."

We just stood there like two total idiots for a few seconds until finally he let go of my hand.

"To whom do I have the honour of speaking?"

"Minn." I giggled. The honour? What planet was he from?

"Minn? That's unusual. Short for Miniature?"

"Ha. Ha."

"Minerva?"

"Yuck."

"Do tell!"

"I don't think so."

"Girl of mystery," he said and grinned. His teeth were even and white against the tan of a wind-burned face, a sailor's tan my mother called it. Windburnt Brown. But I could still make out the scattering of freckles across the bridge of his slightly crooked nose. Not unlike mine. His hair was streaked different shades of toffee. He wasn't cute at all, I thought at once. He was probably what Carolina would consider a hunk.

"Don't you want to know my name?"

"Not really," I said.

"Fine. But seeing as I'm the only one your age around here, you might want to at least be polite."

"How old are you?" I sniffed.

"Fifteen."

He thought I was fifteen.

"Well, see you around!" I said and didn't move.

"Well, I've been dismissed then?"

I looked at the ground. He took the hint and slouched away.

I watched until he disappeared around the bend. My heart was doing a drum roll.

Eventually I looped back to Harvey's Fuel-Up and General Store. Even though my money was back at the house, I figured Harvey would have some Gatorade he'd put on credit. At the very least, I could get a drink of water.

In front of the store was a truck that made me stop in my tracks and almost jump out of my tracksuit. "Cloud Nine Carpet Cleaners." Why was it that clouds were everywhere? Even though I was overheated, I got cold to my bones and rushed past the truck. I flew through the door, ringing the little bells overhead loud as church bells on a Sunday morning.

— THE CLOUDS AGAIN —

Harv's store is a cross between an old-time general store, a hardware store and a convenience store. He sells fishing tackle, hunting gear, gardening equipment and cooking supplies. Pots and pans hang from the ceiling, and Mason jars for pickles and jams are stacked willy-nilly in the corner. Miniature plastic lighthouses, lobster salt and pepper shakers, *Bluenose* key chains and other Nova Scotia souvenirs are displayed next to a counter where he sells fresh fish. A few years back Harv put in new stand-up freezers and now there is all sorts of frozen stuff too, like Sara Lee cakes and TV dinners and even packaged fish and chips.

"For crying out loud, frozen fish in a fishing village, Harv, who's ever going to buy that?" my grandmother asked him at the time.

"Fishermen," Harv replied. "You'd be surprised, Ida, what a treat it can be."

He also rents videos and video games. Then there's the books! His is the only bookstore in the county. He has everything from the latest potboilers to the classics and Oprah's book club picks.

"Well, whoever heard of this—a fish store and bookstore all in one?" I heard a tourist say last year. "Just wait till I write home about this."

"La-di-da!" snapped my grandmother, loud enough for them to hear. "Uppity CFA's. Nothing better to amuse themselves with than going on about how quaint we all are."

CFA's stands for Come From Aways. Nana has no time for them. A friendly woman once told her how hospitable everyone was in Boulder Basin. My grandmother smiled and said, "Well that's because we know you're not staying." I've heard my mother tell that story many times. If Nana thought for a minute anyone was poking fun at the ways of Boulder Basin folks, she'd go on a rant about "those foolish tourists who pay an arm and a leg for stinky lobster traps and strap 'em to the roof of their cars and take them home for coffee tables and planters. Now that's what I call quaint, eh?"

Once she wagged her finger at my nose and said, "Hope you never forget where you come from and go getting too big for your bootstraps, Minn. Just because you live in the city doesn't make you any better than the rest of us."

There she was, one more time, accusing me of something and I'd never even said a word.

As usual, Marie was doing cash. There was no sign of Harv, so I poked around in the book section. He has used books, too. My favourites. Sometimes when I opened one, the pages were so brittle, I was afraid they would crack. They were a tea-stained colour and smelled like attics and rain. Old books have such a mystery about them. I always wondered who belonged to them once. Like who turned the pages before me, drinking in all the words I was reading? I loved to read the notes people sometimes scribbled in the margins.

A blue book on the bottom shelf caught my eye: *The Collected Works of Percy Bysshe Shelley*. I reached for it as someone else did. I jumped. Not before I'd snatched the book myself.

"You like poetry?" His voice was hoarse. I turned and looked into his eyes. Those eyes.

I ignored him. I might have said, I don't! I like, um . . . mystery and adventure. Novels. With endings. Poetry? It sort of leaves you hanging like you're on the edge of a cliff or something and I don't always get it. But I couldn't speak.

"You following me or something?" he said.

I rolled my eyes and looked down at the book, turned pages like a speed reader.

"Stop! Here's my favourite," he said. He leaned over me. He smelled like fresh salt air. He pointed to the title.

"'The Cloud,'" I read. Shivers up and down my neck!
His hand brushed mine. I darn near fainted.

"*Min*-u-et?"

He was way more handsome than Gavin.

"Nuh-uh," I squeaked.

At the till, Marie was pretending to read the tabloid
but I know she was watching every move we made.

"Do you want to know my name yet?" His whisper
tickled the nape of my neck.

I shook my head but I caved in a bit, trying to hide a
smile.

He shrugged. "See ya around." He wandered over to
the video section.

"Gotta run!" I yelled to Marie. "Tell Harv I took a
Gatorade?" I scooted out of there like a bat out of . . .
Tuktoyaktuk.

Minuet? Give me a break.

"I hope you always keep your head on straight when
it comes to boys." Corporal Ray's words echoed from
out of nowhere. My head, at the moment, was lopsided. I was dizzy. So I pushed the thoughts I was
having away.

"Save the Grave, Save the Grave." Nana's words kept
flashing through my head like a blinking neon sign as I
ran all the way to the house. I looked out to sea.

I am positive I heard the screams of drowning people.
Help!

I saw my mother's face before me. I heard her singing a Ladybugs song.

I slammed the door shut behind me, leaned on it as if I could shut out everything. The phone rang and brought me back to earth with a thud.

"Hey, Minn, how's it going?" It was Corporal Ray.

"Fine" is all I said.

"And your grandmother?"

"Same as always," I snorted.

"Are you getting on?"

"Oh yeah, as long as we stay out of one another's way." I wanted him to feel good and guilty.

"Minn, make an effort, all right?"

"How's Mum?"

"Well, we've had a rough couple of days, but we did it."

"Did what?"

"Cleaned out the baby's—"

"Oh. Yeah."

Then he told me that Mr. Forest had an angina attack and the ambulance had to come get him and he was fine but needed to take it easy. Also, Carolina dropped by, lonesome for me but pleased as punch she had a summer job babysitting the Fenton kids and a letter was in the mail.

"Your mother wants to say hello to you," he said. I pictured her by his side, waiting to get on.

"She does?"

There was a sound like he was covering the mouth-
piece.

"Okay, here she is."

"Minn?"

"Mum!"

"Is everything down there okay?"

"Yeah."

"You sure?"

"Yeah."

"Honey, I had this awful dream about you."

"I'm fine, Mum."

"Don't go near the water, okay?" Her voice was urgent. I
could almost see her talking through clenched teeth, her
neck muscles tight. Seemed she pepped up a bit since I left.

"Oookay," I said.

"Good. Well."

"Mum, I saw the most incredible sunrise this morning, you would have loved it—almost like watermelon."

"That's nice, dear," she said, back to that flattened-out
voice I knew so well by now.

"She's tired, Minn." It was Dad again.

"I know, Dad, but when is she ever *not* going to be tired?"

"Time is all she needs," he said, "and rest." I almost
said if she got any more rest she'd turn into some dog
that slept on the front porch with his tongue hanging
out on hot summer days.

"Will she really, Dad? Get better?"

"Cross my heart," he said. But he didn't say *hope to die stick a needle in my eye.* This made me suspicious. Like he was hoping too but didn't know anything for sure.

"Bye, Dad." I had to hang up fast before I told him the truth about how I was.

That I was afraid and lonely and they both seemed to be worlds away from me.

I went to my room and reached beneath my pillow. The skull was smooth, satiny even, like the binding on an old woollen blanket. There was still a tingle on my skin. A kind of feathery whispery feeling that started up the second I looked into the eyes of Beach Boy at the store. He barely even touched me and my heart had flipped. I shivered and stretched. I went out for another run.

⬱ Shipmates ⬱

On the second day at sea, the *Atlantic* docked in Queenstown, Ireland, to pick up more passengers. My father was thrilled to glimpse his "native shores" again—the first time since he'd left.

"There's the Emerald Isle. There's your roots, boys. In that soil there."

"Sounds like we're trees." Thomas was still grumpy.

"I've always felt the luck of the Irish in my veins, Dad," I said, trying to buffer Tom's snub. Things were still tense between them. Dad ruffled my hair. Thomas skulked away.

After the Irish boarded, the ship crackled with laughter. There was singing and dancing and Irish whiskey flowing. A burly man named George supervised rearranging tables and chairs in the dining hall after supper. Musicians were everywhere: fiddlers and accordion players, Irish drums and ten-penny whistles.

Thomas and I hung back at first, watching the older folks.

"Want a sip?" A boy my age held out a bottle. "The name's Ryan," he said, even after I nodded no. Thomas took him up on his offer, though. He ducked behind a post so our folks wouldn't see.

"Where are your parents?" Thomas asked.

"My mother's dead and my father's a drunk," shouted Ryan over the din. "I worked and saved and if I hadn't come up with the money I would have stowed away. But my uncle Danny, who lives in New York, sent me the rest of my fare."

I thought of Michael and his stowaway dreams. Thomas was thinking of his Rebecca, no doubt.

Ryan's accent was thick and at times he was impossible to make out. It didn't matter much. He was like a gulp of fresh air. He had us laughing in no time and soon I was sipping the ale too.

A few hours later I thought I was seeing things. A vision is what I'd call her. Yes, she was a dream. Everything was getting blurry on me by that time, of course. I rubbed my eyes. But no, there she was again. Thomas and Ryan were out on the floor dancing with two girls. I was standing alone. Or rather, trying to stand. And this beautiful vision—this young lady—came right over and smiled at *me*.

"You . . . look a bit green," she said.

"Yes, miss," is all I said.

She was older than Thomas. And more beautiful the closer she came. She smelled like wet rose petals.

"Would you like to get some fresh air?"

"Yes, miss," I said again.

"Are you alone?" she asked.

"Yes, miss."

"Well, let's get you out on deck quickly, shall we?"

"Yes, miss."

I vomited over the railing on the outside deck. She dabbed my mouth with a lace handkerchief. Then she put something underneath my nose that jolted me.

"Smelling salts," she said. "Can't have you fainting on me!"

Thomas and Ryan came out on the deck.

"Do you know his name?" she asked them, as if I wasn't there. I guess I really wasn't either. I couldn't find my tongue to speak.

"John Hindley. I'm Thomas. I'm his brother."

"And I'm Ryan," said Ryan. "And I'm not."

"I am Miss Maryanna Rayborn. And shame on you two. You should take better care of your brother!"

They gawked at her.

"Yes, miss," they chimed in unison.

And then they bowed. Bowed! I never knew Thomas to bow before.

"But she had this way of looking at us," Thomas told me later, "like we should almost kneel before her. Like she was royal almost, not snooty but you know—a lady. And she nodded—friendly enough—but turned her back on us and looked right at you and said, 'Well, John Hindley, my name is Maryanna Rayborn in case you didn't catch that, and I might have to be your guardian angel on board if you're under the charge of these scallywags.' And you said, 'Yes, miss,' and kissed her hand!"

"I did not!"

"Did too!"

I never knew for sure if they were pulling my leg or not.

Apparently, after Miss Rayborn said good night, they carried me to the cabin and helped me climb up into my bunk. I do remember them half laughing and bumping their heads as I fell asleep.

I prayed for sleep before I was sick again.

I dreamt of a woman with green eyes and a white dress made of feathers.

∾ Guided Tour ∾

"The secret is to eat tiny bits all day instead of big meals all at once. And no spirits would help!" Mum scowled at all three of us.

Dad winked at us. "Eyes at the back of her head."

"As if we didn't know!" I said.

"We are in the bowels of the ship," Dad explained, "in what is called the steerage section. This makes the seasickness worse, for sure."

"That explains the smell, then," smirked Thomas. "And here I've been thinking it was your bowels stinking me out, John."

It was cramped, all right. Thomas and I shared a berth in the men's quarters. There was just enough room for our beds, stacked one on top of the other. We argued over who slept on top and decided to take turns. Thomas let me get the upper bunk for the first half of the trip. Although I promised, I wasn't ready to switch with him. I liked being as high up as I could be. All that ocean beneath me was unsettling.

During the day Ryan kept us busy. One morning, he pestered the first mate, a gruff fellow by the name of Frith, until he finally paid us attention.

"How many times you crossed this ocean?"

Frith snorted, and then looked us over as if we were a bother.

"Well, I started at about your age."

"Really?"

"Yes, times were different then. Young boys knew what it meant to put in an honest day's work."

"I'm used to work," Thomas piped up. "Worked at the cotton mill in Ashton until we sailed."

"I'm very busy right now," Frith said. "But come with me. I want to show you young men something."

He led us through three narrow passageways, each one a level lower than the one before. We tunnelled lower and lower. I got this terrible closed-in feeling. Frith chattered on the whole time.

"Imagine now, boys, this ship carries 11,016 pounds of flour, 4,560 pounds of beef, 256 pints of milk, seven gallons of whiskey. That's for starters. Then there's fresh water and butter, port wine and tea—288 pounds of tea. The English and Irish and their tea!"

He gestured to the left and right, pointing things out. Our heads were spinning. Frith called the ship a "she," as if it was a beautiful and powerful woman.

I thought of Miss Maryanna Rayborn.

At the end of each tunnel was a door, securely fastened with clips at the top.

"These are airlocks, boys. Nothing can get through them when they're bolted shut. Are you sure you want to go on?"

I sure wasn't.

"Move on," urged Thomas. But even Ryan's wise-cracking manner had disappeared.

"Mum would have a fit if she knew what we were doing," I whispered to Thomas.

"She doesn't, though," he hissed back, and the sound echoed all around us. Finally, we made it to the bottom of the ship and a final door.

"Behold, young sirs, you're now looking as close as you'll ever get to the mouth of Hades itself," said Frith, and he flung open the door.

"Whooah!" Ryan blew the sound out between clenched teeth and whistled.

"Crikey!"

"Take a gander over there, John Hindley."

The clang of metal and spitting of steam from the boilers beat out a steady thudding rhythm. Below us, throngs of soot-faced, bare-chested men, sweat running in rivers down their backs, shovelled lumps of coal into the furnaces. Even covered with all that grime, they looked to me like ghosts. As the fires lit up, they lit up themselves. It wasn't that much of a stretch to imagine that we were in the Devil's Den.

"She's still a ship that'll travel under wind and sail," Frith was saying, "and for my money that's how I'd sail her if I was the captain. Relying on the likes of these men to do their work is taking a chance. We found fourteen stow-aways when we left Liverpool. Fourteen—that's a record, for sure. Hardly a one of them is useful enough to work one honest shift."

The shouts of the men were lost in the din. One man with biceps hard as anvils barked up at us.

"First Officer Frith, all respect to you, sir, but the boys ain't allowed here." He frowned and jerked his thumb.

Frith waved, but let us stand there a few more moments. We were spellbound by the flickering shadows dancing on the rows of twisted pipes and tubing.

Thomas's eyes were as shiny as the flames themselves. He was breathing hard and grinning from ear to ear. I was breathing hard too but wishing like anything I was on dry land. Still, I pretended for his sake that the whole thing was a great adventure. It was like I had my real brother back again. He slapped my back in his old good-natured way as we headed up the stairwell.

Once back on the upper deck, Frith gave us each a length of rope.

"Now this ain't to be going and hanging yourself with, boys. If you ever plan on being decent sailors, first off, you got to know your knots. Lives can be saved with rope and knots. I'll show you some over the next few days, give you something to pass the time. We'll start with the bowline knot. Simple and strong."

His hands moved so quickly it was hard to follow. This way, that way, criss-crossing. He laughed at our butter-fingered attempts and the looks on our faces when we ended up tangled. So he did it again, much slower this time, working the rope up through the loop of a number six and back in and over.

"Practice makes perfect," he said, and then he was off.

My brother nudged Ryan. "Shall we go and find Emily and Sara?" They must be the two they'd been trying to impress the night before. Girls again!

"Thought you left your heart back in England," I teased.

"Shut your mouth," Thomas snapped.

Ryan perked right up. "What's this?"

"Thomas is heartsick, don't you know?" I had to duck and run to get out of his reach.

I stood for a long time on deck, looking up into the rigging. The sails were down and the tangles of ropes made me dizzy. The mizzenmast, Frith had told us, was the third mast from the bow. Often a sailor proved his seaworthiness by climbing to the top of one of the masts.

I knew I'd never be a sailor. I was as afraid of heights as I was of depths.

"Something to behold, isn't it, Master Hindley." *Her.*

"Yes, miss."

"Do you know any other words than those?"

"Yes, miss."

Her laughter made me dizzier than the rigging I'd been looking up into.

I laughed too.

"That sure is a long ways up," I said.

"Could you climb it?" she asked.

"That's just what I was wondering."

"What was your conclusion?"

"I thought not."

"Well, I'm a person who thinks you can do anything if you want to. Or have to."

"I don't think I'd ever want to, miss, and unless I become a sailor I won't have to."

"Please call me Maryanna. Miss makes me feel so old. Ma'am is worse! I'm not a married woman yet."

"Yet?"

"That's why I'm sailing. My fiancé is waiting for me on the other side. In New York. I can hardly wait!" She jumped up a little when she said New York.

"Me too," I said. "I mean, I'm going to New York, too! And my brother is going to send for his girl as soon as he can." I brought up Thomas to make her know how well I understood love and passion.

"And you? No broken heart you left behind?"

I shook my head.

"Well, then. We'll just have to keep each other good company, won't we?"

She linked her arm in mine. I nodded like a fool.

I think Miss Rayborn was lonely. I was just a young boy to her. She probably had no idea how she affected me.

At that moment I needed another dose of those smelling salts.

❧ What Parents Do ❧

"I don't care if the king of England himself were sitting with us. When it's time for a mother to speak, it has to be done."

Sure enough, Mum had found out where we'd been. Thomas couldn't help spilling the beans to Dad. Dad was right proud and boasted to everyone. What was he thinking?

Mum scowled. "Boys, over here, please, so the whole world won't hear everything."

We obeyed.

"Mr. Ryan O'Brien, that means you as well! Seeing as you're their mate this trip and I wouldn't mind having a handsome son like you anyhow, especially with that talent for laugh. But it goes with trouble, too.

"Now. Don't you go pulling any shenanigans like that again. Dig the earwax out and hear me good, because I mean it." She twisted our ears as she spoke.

"Ow."

"Woah!"

"Mum!"

But truth be told, we were all trying not to laugh. Mum could twist hard enough to make it sting, but mostly it was never more than a pinch. She was such a biddy thing, and now that we were all taller than her, she had to stand on her tiptoes to wag a finger in our face.

"I can just imagine the language coming out of those men down there was not fit for any civilized gentleman."

"I'm not so civilized as all that, Mum," Thomas mumbled. "Heard worse at the mill, you know, every single day."

"Well, good sir, man of the world, are you? So maybe there's little hope for you, but your brother here is about to be an educated gentleman. He won't be having any need for that sort of filth."

"Yes, Ma. Sorry, Mum."

It was true, my schooling was one of the main reasons Dad decided to leave Lancashire county and head off to New York.

"A boy like you to whom reading comes so easily needs more schooling, not the mill." He'd said this the first time I came home from school and recited some little poem for them after supper one evening. It was something I was asked to do regularly, for entertainment on winter nights. But it was my last year of public school. There was no money for more, not back home in England. In America, I could continue school for free.

"Yes," Dad said to me the night he told me of his plans. "You'll get a better life than your old man's, eh?" I knew what he meant, but the thing of it was, if I was to grow up to be a man like him, that would please me well enough.

"To Paddy, the man with a ready laugh and a huge heart and the strongest arms in the mill," said the fellows when they lifted pints to him on the night of their farewell party. And that described him, all right. Yes, indeed. Patrick Hindley was the kind of man any son would be proud to grow up to be.

— DIRTY OLD GEEZERS —

The water was cold. The pipes clanged in protest as I refilled my glass. I stood at the kitchen window as I sipped it, staring up at the hill. And right then, Beach Boy appeared out of nowhere and waved at me to join him. The glass slid out of my hand and shattered into a bazillion pieces on the tile floor. A shard of glass pricked my finger as I swept it into the dustpan, and blood spurted out like a mini geyser. After doctoring myself up, I started up the hill.

Burdock stuck to my socks, thistles scratched my ankles, and I had to thread carefully through tangles of spiderwebs. Fat spiders with yellow and black bodies sat content in the middle of lacy designs spread between the tips of timothy, like blankets at a picnic. I hate spiders. Still, I climbed.

"Hey!" I bellowed out to the sky and the wind. "Are you here?"

The sea crashed on the rocks below and eddied back out. My voice echoed back. *Here, here, here.* The gulls screeched, and from the other side of the basin came the low groan of a motorboat put-putting towards the government dock.

I spotted Nana's truck pulling into the driveway and I dove down, hoping the grass hid me.

"Minn!" she called towards the house. "Come help me lug in these berries."

I flattened myself farther into the grass, waited until she'd gone in for the last time and then rolled over. The clouds were silvery white; the sky filled with scribbled chalky lines and shapes. I thought of hieroglyphs in ancient caves. Dinosaur, dolphin, castle, face of bear. After the morning's workout, it was a perfect place to rest.

"Ida!" Harv's voice interrupted my daydreams. I leaned up on my elbows to watch.

Nana came out of the house with two glasses of lemonade. Harv took them from her and placed them on the table. Then, to my disgust, they embraced. And worse, they kissed—like lovers kiss. Tongue and everything, it looked like. Gross.

They sat down and sipped their lemonade. A romance between Harv and my grandmother! Ew. Imagine what they'd be up to if I wasn't around to cramp their style! Ew. Ew. Ew. Did my father know about this? Come to think of it, Harv did come with us last year to the Herring

Choker Picnic and the potluck at the church.

Well, well. My grandmother and Harv. So much for Alex Trebek.

On the way down the hill, I hummed loud enough to give them plenty of warning in case they had any idea of giving in to their passion and making out. Dirty old geezers!

"Here's the girl herself now," said Harv as I walked up the steps.

"Strawberries in the kitchen need hullin'," said my grandmother.

"Just a minute now, Ida. I brought your granddaughter a gift, I did."

He reached inside the large pocket of his lumberjack shirt and produced the book I'd been looking at in his store.

"Marie says you took a real interest in this. I want you to have it."

"Thanks, Harv," I said.

"She said you were acting sort of strange. And . . ." He paused. *Don't please don't say anything about the boy.* He winked. "And you owe me a Gatorade." *Whew.* "And . . . she said you took off like a bat outta hell!"

"Harv!" Nana barked like a teacher.

"Excuse me. Like a bat out of Tutuyukytuk!

I knew it! Marie the checkout girl had ears and eyes like a hawk! She'd been checking me out, all right.

"It was just that I remembered Dad was going to call this morning and I didn't want to miss it."

"What'd he have to say?" asked Nana.

"Nothing much."

"Do Eaton's tell Sears their business?" Harv asked her.

"Eaton's went *out* of business, last I heard," snapped Nana.

"Got me there," sighed Harv.

"How's your mother?" Nana continued, one eyebrow arching up high. It was the first time she'd mentioned her. Maybe she figured I'd talk to her more in front of Harv. That his being there would force me to be polite.

"The same," I mumbled, flipping through the book so I wouldn't have to look her in the eye.

"She'll be fine, I'm sure she will," said Nana. Almost, I realized with a shock, almost as if she was trying to make me feel better. Sure, put on a show for your lover, so he won't know what a witch you are.

"Whatever," I said, and went into the house, letting the screen door slam behind me.

I expected her to shout out not to be so rude, but she stayed on her sweet as opposed to sour behaviour at the moment.

I threw the book on my bed, peeled off my sweaty clothes and went to shower. I should have waited until after hulling the berries, because my fingers were stained red and my fingernails almost purple by the time I was through. It looked like I'd been splashing my hands in a puddle of blood.

Later that afternoon, Nana turned on the radio and we listened to the CBC as we mixed the biscuits for the strawberry shortcake.

"Harv's coming over for dessert," she announced. I bet he is, I wanted to say.

"He loves his strawberry shortcake, all right," she said, "with real whip cream, though, not that artificial stuff that makes your teeth rot. Here, you can lick the beaters if you want."

Supper was delicious, a feast of boiled potatoes, fresh peas, hot German sausages and sauerkraut. I left plenty of room for dessert.

"Now Shelley, he was a great poet," said Harv afterwards, as he puffed on his pipe. "His life was too short and he would have written more poems, I am sure, that we'd still be remembering today."

"Maybe not," said Nana, puffing on her pipe as well. "Sometimes the best poetry is written in the prime of one's life, in youth, when the emotions are still not in check and passions are high."

"Are you saying old folks don't have high passion?" I blurted.

Nana flushed and Harv nearly choked on his smoke.

"Well!" said Nana.

"I saw you two smooching on the porch this afternoon," I teased.

Harv laughed. "Well, well, Ida, I guess our little secret is out."

"Nosy little thing. It's not polite to be spying on people." Nana pouted like a kid.

"But I wasn't spying," I protested between my giggles. "I just happened to look down at the wrong time."

This was fun, seeing her all kafuffled.

"I'd like to marry your grandmother," said Harv like a courtly gentleman. "But she won't have me."

"Harv, now don't start in," warned my grandmother, her face almost as purple as an eggplant.

"Yup. Guess she thinks an old guy would only be getting in her way all the time."

"Well, I do like my freedom," sniffed Nana. "Besides, they'd only cut my old age pension, and a woman needs her own woodpile."

"But I'm not a poor man exactly, Ida," said Harv. There was weariness in his voice. I guessed they'd been over this a lot of times.

"Your family would not approve," she said. "Probably call me a gold digger."

"My children would be tickled pink, Ida. You know that!"

"That's what you think now, Harv, but believe me, it's a different story when the time comes."

I think for a minute they forgot I was there as they squabbled like two old crows.

"Minn," said Harv suddenly, as if he could read my thoughts, "you'd come to the wedding, wouldn't ya?"

"I'd sing at it if I could sing," I said. Then I began my own rendition of "Ave Maria." The one with Corporal Ray's country-and-western twang.

"Stop!" My grandmother covered her ears, laughing. "Lordie, that's a good enough reason to never say yes."

It seemed she was leaving the door open a bit.

I have to admit that knowing Harv loved my grandmother and wished to marry her painted her in a whole new light for me. Harv was a great guy. Even when I was little I knew he was a kind man. There's a twinkle in certain grown-ups' eyes that little kids know means this is a grown-up you can trust. And when they say "how are you?" they really mean *who* are you, and you know they want an answer. A real one, not just "fine, thank you."

"Well, I'll do the dishes and give you two lovebirds time alone," I said.

"Now I'm going to have to put up with this foolishness from here on in, I suppose," muttered Nana. "And don't be saying anything to your father, do you promise me?"

Ha, just as I suspected.

"My lips are sealed," I said. "For now."

They sat on the veranda until well after dark. I went to bed and read Mr. Shelley's poems until I fell asleep.

Not before I remembered to do the Rigbyism exercise, though. By this time, I had myself coming in fourth, and although I was still wearing the letter carrier's uniform, the shoulder bag was gone. But waiting for me at the finish line was none other than Gavin turned into Beach Boy. Arms outstretched, white teeth gleaming, ready to hug me and swirl me in the air. Coach Rigby would probably say this was progress. I felt like I was turning into Carolina. Never had a boy so invaded my every waking moment.

I decided to consult an expert. I tore a page out of my journal.

> *Dear Carolina:*
> *Would you say when your mouth fills up with cotton*
> *and you feel like you're gonna gag and your heart does*
> *the rumblemombo and there's this clammy feeling*
> *behind your kneecaps that it's LUV? Just askin.*
> *Minn*

I scrunched it up and threw it in the corner of my room. I did twenty-seven push-ups and twenty-nine jumping jacks and felt not one bit better.

— NEWS FROM HOME —

A routine settled in over the next week or so. From sun-up to midday, Nana was rooted in her herb garden like a bad weed. I trained like a demon. In the afternoons, I read while she went to her room to "rest for a spell." But she usually dozed off, snoring louder than a tractor. Escape time! I would wander down to the shore. My search for heart-shaped rocks continued, but truth is, I hoped to find more bones. Even better, I wanted some treasure from the wreck to wash up on shore. Valuable treasure. I'd call the media. I could see the headlines now: "No Oak Island Treasure but Boulder Basin Riches Uncovered by Budding Archaeologist." My picture would appear beneath it. A flattering picture. I would grant an interview, which would spark interest in the grave.

But no luck. No rocks, no bones and no treasure. No Hardly Whynot sighting. I'd never make detective, and some archaeologist I was.

A gravesite was still washing out to sea.

Every afternoon, I had to help Nana prepare supper. I shelled peas until I saw green, diced onions until no tears were left and peeled a truckload of potatoes. Nana loved leftovers. It meant no work for lunch the next day. Mostly, we worked in silence. Sometimes, she'd mutter on to herself about an article in *National Geographic*. All I'd have to say is, "Oh really?" and she'd elaborate forever. But I didn't listen. I was doing my Rigbyism exercises the whole time. This caused some awkward moments.

"I tasted some once, right off the bark of a tree in Zanzibar."

"What? You ate tree bark?"

"In Zanzibar. Real cinnamon. Never tasted anything like that from a bottle."

"Oh." She'd once gone on an exchange teaching trip to Africa. I figured she'd scared her students to death.

On top of the piano was a picture of her in Africa. She dusted it every day. In this picture, there were no students. She was kissing a hippopotamus. On the nose. A baby hippopotamus. The poor hippo.

"Do you like them?" She was still prattling away.

"Pardon me?"

"Cinnamon buns. I asked you if you liked the buns you were named after."

"Yes."

"Well, then," she said, "watch and learn. I'll show you how they're done."

She was a whiz with the dough. She let me sprinkle on the cinnamon and sugar and let me roll it sideways. When I was little, my mother used to let me do the same. After the age of nine, I avoided the kitchen whenever I could. Now I felt guilty. All the hours I might have spent with my mother when she was still a human being. But no, I was too busy off doing something more important with Carolina.

"The recipe was mine to begin with," Nana snapped when I told her hers were good but not quite the same as my mother's. "She probably adds more sugar," she said more gently when she saw my face. Thoughts of my mother were needle pricks in the pin cushion of my heart. I refused the buns after that.

"Want to splurge?" she asked the next night. She grabbed the keys to her truck. "Come on!"

We hopped in the truck and drove ten minutes down the road to the Windjammer Restaurant for fried clams and chips. I couldn't help but notice she liked vinegar on her fries. She cracked a few lame jokes. She was obviously trying as hard as she could to be as nice as possible to me. It must have taken enormous effort. Keeping my own harbour of hate under control was exhausting.

Beach Boy joined me on several morning runs. I discovered he was left-handed. That was about it. Mostly, I lost my voice around him. And he continued his guessing game.

"Min-i-van? Min-i-mum? Min-i-skirt?" and on he'd go.

"I'll tell you if you tell me," I said.

"Honest?"

"Cross my heart," I said. But I crossed my fingers behind my back.

"Max. Your turn."

"Sta-MIN-a!" I shouted and sprinted ahead of him.

"No fair!" he gasped. "But I didn't trust you anyhow! Max is *not* my real name."

"Well, Max is tickety-boo with me! As in Max-imum loser! You a *looosah*! Me a *winnah*!" I left him sputtering and choking on my dust. I'm not sure he appreciated my humour. I was only imitating Coach Rigby. *Be a winnah, not a loosah!*

Harv came over most nights. Sometimes Nana played the piano. Boooring. Mostly hymns. Sometimes they listened to records by Nat King Cole. More boooring. But sometimes, if I asked, Harv told stories. Or read to us from Mr. Shelley. Harv's voice was like gentle thunder. When he got going, it boomed out, echoing across the water and back again. Sometimes, although I can't explain why, the poems almost brought tears to my eyes. Half the time I didn't know the meaning of the words, but there was something about their music,

rippling through the darkness, that I seemed to understand all the same. For a second, a flick of a firefly light,
everything felt fine.

I was on my second Rigbyism—one entirely the
opposite from the first:

> *The start of each race is where the race can be won or*
> *lost. Close your eyes and picture yourself warming up*
> *before the race. Do not—I repeat—do not look your*
> *opponent in the eyes. This game of psyching each other*
> *out is, in my mind, nothing but a waste of energy. This*
> *is about you and the best you can do, not about them at*
> *all. Instead, focus your eyes down the track towards the*
> *finish line. Start mentally seeing yourself exploding*
> *from the starting blocks. Get your feet positioned. The*
> *starter's voice begins, on yer mark, now rise up, get set,*
> *and hear the blast of that pistol! You're off! First one out*
> *of the gate! Over and over again—BEGIN your race.*

So I did. There was the lime on my fingers like fine
white powder and the gravelly smell of the track, a little
like tar. But every time—false start! I was disqualified,
finished before I started. That's what a loser I was.
Loosah! Loosah! This exercise was not calming, either. My
heart raced like it did in a real sprint. The darkness
seemed to press in on my chest, and thoughts of Beach
Boy spun like a whirlpool in my clogged-up head.

I got a letter from Carolina that made me realize how badly I needed to talk to someone.

Dear Girlfriend:

Whassup? Miss you loads, kiddo. Got myself a job supervising the tot lot program at the park in the mornings and babysitting the Fenton kids in the afternoon. It's all right, I suppose. All the kids pee in the pool and last week little Roddy Foreman who goes in with his diaper on left a banana-sized turd floating around in the water. It emptied the pool so fast you would have thought it was full of sharks. It was disgusting. I scooped the poop out with someone's sand shovel. Saved the day!

The Fenton kids are okay . . . pretty whiny by the end of the day . . . but the money's worth it. I'm saving up for a new CD player.

I saw Gavin once. I dithered and dathered before deciding to tell you. But then I thought I wouldn't be a friend if I didn't. If it were me, I'd want you to tell me. So here's the bad news. I saw him holding hands with that rat-face Heather McDorman and word has it they're going together. Sorry. Hope your heart's not broken or anything and you don't hate me for telling you the bad news. Anyhow, I nearly scratched out her eyes on your behalf. The way I figure it, if he couldn't wait for you to come back it wasn't meant to be and

he's not worth your energy. Right? Anyhow, I know
now I won't be able to visit because of my jobs and all
but I'm thinking of you loads and miss you like
crazee. Hugs and kisses pal o' mine.

Carolina

The news about Gavin stung for a bit, I'll admit. Just
a sting, though. It didn't last long. Just a day or two. No
worse than a jellyfish sting.

∼ Man Almost Overboard ∼

You learn a lot about the folks you call your shipmates. We bumped into each other in the stairwells and passages. We took turns passing the buckets into which we had all been sick at least once. Folks made real friends with each other— most folks, at least. A few found it best not to be in each other's company for too long.

"It's only human," Dad said. "Not all of us can take to each other. Throw a pack of us together and we can be like animals, moving together in the pack, then sometimes, for no reason, some attack each other. And some are the lone ones circling outside, never sure where they fit in or if they even do."

But usually, come evening, everyone was feeling festive. Ryan surprised us one night and took the spotlight. He did this step-dance routine he'd worked out with the fiddler. He called it "Mister, Can I Have Another Pint?" As the music sped up, his legs wobbled more and more.

"It's like his legs have lost all the bones," squealed Mum, clapping.

He bowed low when he was done and passed his hat.

"I'll have a wad by the time we hit New York! Someday, I'm gonna take myself to Mr. P. T. Barnum's spectacle, is what I'm going to do. Ever heard of it? Giants and ladies with beards and weird and weirder things! Maybe someday you folks'll catch my act there!"

"No. And I meant no!" It was Miss Maryanna Rayborn. She was in the corner, fending off a man by the name of Mr. Thaddeus Redman. He would be the lone wolf Dad spoke of. In the blink of an eye men ran to her rescue, including my father.

"Is this man bothering you, Miss Rayborn?" Dad asked her.

"Yes. He made lewd and improper suggestions I have not invited."

She was her usual composed self. Mr. Redman was holding his private parts. And moaning.

"I'm afraid I had to resort to some violence." She held up her parasol. The men all winced.

Dad and several other men lifted Redman up by the arms and legs.

"Shall we heave him overboard, then, lads?" Dad said.

Amidst the laughing, a very red-faced Mr. Redman was escorted out of the dining hall.

"This'll be your only warning," yelled Dad. He returned

to applause, and Miss Rayborn joined us at our table. I could barely breathe.

"John and I have met already," she informed my mother.

"I see," said Mum. "John, you never told me." She raised her eyebrows in mock surprise.

"I expect there's so much excitement on board for a fellow his age, he forgot all about me."

How wrong she was. I hadn't been thinking about much else. I'd been following the lingering smell of wet rose petals all over the ship.

I knew now I had a glimmer of how Thomas felt about Rebecca. No wonder he twitched so much.

∼ Performance ∼

Folks were tuckered out from partying the night before. The atmosphere on board was all whispers; a hush had settled over us. We'd been told we had to make an unexpected stop next day in Canada to take on more coal.

"I was telling you, wasn't I," Frith said, shaking his head, "that sail was always the best way to go. None of this stopping over in places we don't have to case we run short. So much for the modern way of doing things."

"Bloody hell," he said. "Excuse my language, lads." He scratched those white whiskers of his, tough as broom bristles, and gave one of his snorts. "Ah well, I suppose another two days won't matter that much though, eh?"

He was dead wrong. For most of us, one day seemed like a fortnight. We weren't seafaring folks like him. A day was an eternity at this point. No wonder things were so sombre.

Ryan and Thomas were the exceptions. They figured two more days gave them more time to get chummy with Emily and Sara. They were off somewhere with them and I was alone. Again. Except not really *that* alone. I had several conversations with Miss Maryanna. She asked me questions, and though I could barely whisper in her presence I told her things. Such as what I wanted to do when I grew up.

"A writer or a teacher," I said.

"A writer! How romantic!" she said and grabbed my arm. And started to tell me all about her wedding plans. Definitely a writer, I thought, if that was the reaction of a beautiful woman. Mind you, little good it did when they were off to marry another. But I did have a friend in her. I had never told anyone those things before. I like to think she favoured me, but truth is, whenever I saw her with anyone else, she had that same smile and nod. You could tell they thought they were the most fascinating person in the world at that moment.

So Thomas and Ryan had girlfriends. I had a lady friend.

"Those girls would drive me foolish enough after a bit," I muttered to Dad. "And what about Becca?"

"Sit," said Dad.

We played a game of whist as a few musicians started up.

Then there she was. Miss Maryanna Rayborn had recovered from the previous night. Someone persuaded her to sing. Her voice was like a dream of angels singing. She sang a sad, sweet song, blushed, and when everyone clapped, she curtsied modestly. Even from where I sat, I heard the folds of her dress rustle around her. A green dress to match those eyes of hers. They were sparkling as she looked around the room as if searching for someone. She was still up on the stage the musicians had built from wooden potato crates. Finally, her bewitching eyes settled on me.

"John Hindley! Your mother says you're something of an orator. You've been so quiet all these nights. Perhaps you'll give us a recital, maybe even one of your own, for I understand you're a bit of a young Will Shakespeare!"

"Ma! You did not!" I cringed.

My mother shrugged her shoulders and smirked. "It's true enough, John. A mother can boast if a child has a talent. Besides, when God gives a gift, it's meant to be shared."

I shook my head until shouts from the other passengers echoed around the room.

"Hear, hear, John!"

"Bend our ears, lad!"

"Imagine, a bard amongst us all this time!"

There was no polite way to refuse. Reciting for my school chums and family was no big deal. But this? My knees felt like Ryan's had looked like in his raggedy dance.

I went to the front of the room, took Miss Rayborn's hand and stepped up on the stage. She clapped with the rest, then bent and whispered in my ear—what, I couldn't say. Her closeness seemed to make me deaf as well as dumb. And then she left me alone. I cleared my throat.

"For your pleasure, good sirs and madams, I will recite one of my favourite pieces. It is called 'Bolton's Yard' and is by the Lancashire poet Samuel Laycock. Although I'm from Ashton, it could well have been our neighbourhood Mr. Laycock wrote of."

I did a fine enough job, and there was a silence when I finished the poem. Then the clapping started. "Bravo! Bravo, young John." I saw my mother's beaming face and Dad dabbing at his eyes. As I made my way back to the table I was rewarded with many slaps on the back.

It was a while before I could settle down to sleep that night. The silence that happened before the clapping lingered—for one second it was if all our souls were joined together. It was like nothing I'd ever felt in my life before, being one with so many people.

I was disappointed that Thomas had missed my performance. Plus, it was my turn to sleep in the bottom bunk. I'd been mad at my brother and Ryan most of the day. Ryan beat me when Frith timed us doing our knots that morning. I had bet my best and cleanest pair of socks. What Mum would have to say about gambling like that! Still, it was better than my carving knife. It was a present from Dad my last birthday. It was as beautiful as it was useful. The blade was curved and the handle made of black leather studded with dark green stones. Ryan wanted it, all right. Even Thomas was putting pressure on me to sell it.

"Money talks," he said. "You might need some cash when we get to New York."

"It doesn't talk that loud to me!" I snapped back at them both.

Where on earth was he? I wanted to tell him about my reciting. I wanted to tell him I was sorry for being crabby. It was late. Some companion he turned out to be.

I snatched the top bunk back for my own. Just for spite.

He stumbled in a good thirty minutes later. It was more than ale he'd been drinking. Whisky, from the smell of him. Alcohol fumes filled the cabin.

"Johnnie." Thomas shook me gently. He was trying to whisper but his voice was a saw cutting through the dark. "You're in my bed, you lump of coal, get down, would ya!"

I snored, loud as a bear.

"Sure I know you're awake, now fair is fair and it's my turn."

I was about to jump up and let him have his bed but I heard him flop down on the lower bunk and start snoring for real.

— RUNNING THOUGHTS —

"Why do you like running?" Max asked me.

"I'm in training."

"But why do you like it?"

I shrugged and ran off.

It seemed to me he was asking me about more than running. It was the way he looked, serious like a professor pondering over "the many quandaries of the world," as Harv would say. The unanswerable questions, he meant by that, of which there were more than answered ones. I had a list yay long of my own.

As for the running, the answer was easy enough on mornings when the sun shone down with just enough heat to warm my shoulders and the breeze blew just enough to keep me cool and my legs felt strong and fast, as if they'd fly beneath me forever. I loved kicking up a dust storm behind me on those roads. I imagined myself a young, wild horse that no one could tame.

It was the way the air felt, too. Not just the air blowing around me. It was the sharpness of it—peppermint cool—inside me as I breathed. I sucked that air like drinking pure water straight from a well. And that feeling in my chest as my diaphragm contracted, filling me up with that air. Sometimes, as I ran, I pictured this little army of window cleaners moving through my body, scrubbing it clean with that air after a thick fog of night's sleep had settled in my bones and muscles. It was a wake-up call for the blood to start circulating and my muscles to start moving.

Running gave me a feeling of power. There was no doubt of that. I felt strong, not just on the outside, in my legs and my arms, but I felt strong inside too, as if in running harder and faster, climbing one more steep hill, I could convince myself that I was strong enough to face almost anything in life. Then there was the other way my body felt at certain moments—like my body dropped away and I *was* the wind. I was the road and the sky and the grass and the sea and everything.

"I love running," I should have told him, "because I disappear. I am no longer who I am, but a wisp of wind, a flower dancing its petals in the early-morning breeze, a cloud shifting before your eyes. Weightless. A spirit. Like . . . my *sister*."

Not that I'd ever tell him that. Not that I'd likely have a chance. For a few days, I only saw him in the distance, always going the other way.

— HARDLY SIGHTING —

I focused on my training. I might have stayed focused too, but then it happened. One afternoon, the limousine honked. Mr. Mafia Bodyguard saluted but didn't stop. In the front seat, beside him, was none other than . . . Hardly Whynot! I was almost positive. The provincial record for the hundred metres was shattered that morning as I sped back to Nana's to call Carolina.

"I knew it!" she squealed. "I knew it!"

"I'm not a hundred per cent but—"

"Your mother will be so thrilled! Get me an autograph too, okay? He's old but he's famous." She screamed. "Ohmygawd!"

I said I'd do my best. Then I told her about my discovery of the skull and the story of the shipwreck.

"It's a sign," she said.

"Of what?"

"That you are supposed to be in Boulder Basin—that you're there for a reason."

Carolina and her signs!

"You say the bones from the grave are washing out to sea and up on shore?"

"Yeah."

"And your grandmother thinks something ought to be done?"

"Yeah. And for once, I think she's right, but nobody paid any attention to her when she started trying."

"Was it just her trying?"

"What do you mean?"

"I mean, how many people did she have with her when she went to town council?"

"I think it was just her."

"One little old woman? Look, Minn, people ignore older people and their causes all the time. What she needs is some help. You've heard the expression there's strength in numbers, right? Well, here's what you should do—help her. Get a petition going."

"Petition?"

"Exactly, like the one we did to get new chairs for the cafeteria."

"Carolina, you're a genius."

"Yes, I have been told that often enough. That's why I have such a good job at the moment changing poopy diapers."

We trashed Heather McDorman for a while and had a good laugh. I told her I'd met a boy.

"Is he cute?"

"I dunno."

"Minn?"

"Sort of. I guess. But my mind's on other more important things."

"What's more important than l-u-v?" she said. It was good to hear some things were still the same. By the time I hung up, my petition was already half written.

— SAVE THE GRAVE! —

"Save the Grave!" I wrote in bright orange felt-tip marker. Then I wrote a paragraph explaining the condition of the gravesite and the lives lost on that day, and finished with: "Save the lost souls, add your name below."

The hardest part was to approach Nana. This meant I had to admit that I was interested in the whole thing.

"So," she said after she read it, peering at me fiercely over her glasses. "You're thinking this might help?" She was trying not to look impressed. "Well, well, Walla Walla Washington! A petition, eh? Right proper and all?"

"I thought maybe we could put it on the bulletin board at Harv's store and see what happened?"

"Suppose it wouldn't do any harm to try," she said. "But don't go getting your hopes up. I tell you, people are mostly interested in their own business and things that happen now. They forget that the past was once as real as the present and that one day their future will be past too, that someday they'll be but memories, too. Maybe you got to get old to really know this—how no one wants to be forgotten." She had this faraway look in her eyes.

"I'm not old," I said, "and I think it's important."

"I'll dig out the papers from the bone closet so you can get the facts," she said. As if I needed to read them again.

But I did. I tried to put them in some kind of order. I hung a string across my bedroom and began to paper-clip the articles up like clothes on a line. I put a few of my Rigbyisms there too. Plus I took some paint swatches and made my name. I cut out an M in Bayberry Green. An I in Juniper. An N in Purple Heather. My room needed some colour.

But the coffin-like box that gave me the shivers? I shoved it far to the back of what I considered my treasure drawer. The one that held my mother's paint swatches, a few rocks, my urchin and sand dollar, my journal, my training diary. Ordinary private treasures. Along with the skull.

When I took the petition to the store, Harv got pretty excited. He posted it front and centre of the bulletin board. He shared my grandmother's passion in more ways than one, I guess.

≈ Nightmare ≈

I was dreaming of New York. Again. The city was a dazzle in the sun as the ship sailed into the harbour. A throng of people lined the shore, waving us in. Everyone on board was cheering. There was the victory blast of the ship's horn. Even the air smelled of hope, of newness, like fresh sheets blown dry by wind. This time, the dream was so real, I even felt my sister's arms as she reached out to hug me after we disembarked. Thomas and I helped Dad load the crate and cradle onto a carriage.

Then the Black Knight strolled by. Clang clang clang. Thomas yelled and pointed. The cradle tipped and fell. It made a sound that shuddered through my entire body. I woke with a start. But I wasn't in my bunk. I had been thrown clear through the cabin door.

The cracking sound continued, thunderclaps beneath the ship instead of overhead in the sky. There was a stampede of feet by my head. Men stormed into the passageway.

I staggered to my feet as they elbowed their way past.

"This way, boy, get up on deck." Someone tugged at my sleeve. I pulled away.

"Thomas!" I yelled. I couldn't see my brother in the crowd of bodies pressing around me.

The ship lurched. I fell sideways. I tried to crawl through a tangle of legs back towards the cabin.

"Thomas!"

"Don't go in there boy, don't." But it was too late.

The upper and lower bunks had collapsed in on one another.

"*Thomas!*" I screamed.

My brother's eyes were open, filled with a look of surprise. Unblinking. His head was dangling by a thread of skin.

— LOCAL GOSSIP —

"Know how to slit a dead man's throat?"

I nodded. "Kinda sorta." Corporal Ray's been trying to teach me for years. I'm not very good."

"Come on, Minikin. Give me what you've got." He placed a small round stone in my hand.

"Minikin? Is that a word?"

"Look it up if you don't believe me."

I gave it my best. The rock went up up up then kachunk!

"Not bad for a—" He stopped himself. "But here's how it's done."

He angled his body sideways. Then took a run and flung his arm up.

"Perfect slit, eh what?"

I nodded, impressed. "How did you do that?"

"Years of practice."

"You lived here all your life?"

"Most of it, yes."

"Suppose you know all about the disaster, then?"

He glanced at me. His eyes were hard. "Which one? The Swissair crash a few years ago, down the coast a bit?"

I shuddered. Nana and Harv and most Boulder Basin folks were involved in helping the victims' families. There had been no survivors that night.

"No. This was a shipwreck over a century ago. The SS *Atlantic.*"

"I know a bit." He was skipping rocks by then. He was good at that too.

So I told him about my grandmother and her hope to save the grave. And my petition.

"Minn the gravesaver, eh?"

I shrugged. "The petition's not working. No one signed it yet."

"Why not go door to door? Makes it more personal."

"I don't know anybody, though."

"I'll tell ya what you want to know." He pointed to the house on our left. "Mabel Langille. Never married. When she was little, kids used to call her plug ugly. She was born with a cleft palate. Nicest soul you'd ever want to meet. But folks are cruel. Some folks, anyhow. She's a friend of your grandmother's. Mabel looked after her folks until they died, then took one trip. She went to Niagara Falls. Walks her cat every day. Cat sits on her shoulder and they walk down the beach. Other than that, she doesn't go out much. Other than your grand-mother, she doesn't get much company."

Mabel. Nana had mentioned her but I'd never met her.

Then he pointed to the right. "Roger Verlong. Famous for farting in church."

I burst out laughing.

"I'm serious. Farting or snoring. But again, don't let appearances and gas attacks rule him out. He's a regular teddy bear. A farting, snoring, God-fearing man."

I had to wipe tears of laugher out of my eyes. "We sat right behind the man last Sunday."

"Lucky you!"

"Where do *you* live?" I asked before I even thought the thought.

He pointed. Up, over, up, across. "Near East Boulder."

"Any brothers or sisters?"

He nodded yes. "You?"

"None," I said.

I guess he sensed my irritation.

"Race you to the next birch?"

He beat me for the first time.

"Cnicus benedictus! I guess I better practise harder!"

"I had a head start." It wasn't true. He *was* nice, I decided right then.

"Want to come with me when I take my petition around?" I asked. "Maybe tonight?" What was I doing? Asking him out? *Ditz! I am a total ditz.*

"Terribly sorry. I work at night."

Yeah, like when I saw him walking in the sunset.

"But I'll be with you in spirit." He flashed those pearly whites and put his hand over his heart. "Honest."

≈ APRIL 1ST, 1873 ≈

"Thomas!"

I screamed out my brother's name until my voice was hoarse and my breathing was laboured. I was paralyzed, motionless there on the floor until the ship lurched again. This time it was a long as well as violent shuddering. I was spit back out into the passageway and slammed repeatedly against a wall. Splinters of wood gouged my head and I felt the warm gush of my own blood running down my cheek, into my mouth. There's little doubt I was badly dazed for it was as if the world dropped away suddenly. I was in my body and yet not in my body, like some perplexed and helpless observer watching the bedlam which ensued.

Sounds were muffled and voices warbled much the way it is if ever you have tried to blow bubbles beneath water. Time was no longer time, it was like an accordion. Seconds bent back upon themselves and doubled and then stretched out again. There was such a hurly-burly of men with their

faces contorted and mouths twisted open but all I heard
was a growling, like fierce dogs in a fight. I tried to decipher
the sounds as if translating from a foreign language.

"Out! Now!"

Was that my father's voice? Wherewasmydadmymum?

Someone, but no—not my father, yanked me by the arm
so hard I thought my elbow dislodged from its socket. I
staggered about on my feet but not for long. They lifted me,
a whole line of them, and then thrust me forward, hand
over hand, head over head, until I reached a small porthole
someone had smashed open.

"Heave!" I heard them shout. I closed my eyes as I shot
right through like a canyon ball, exploding out onto what
remained of the deck. Needlepoint slivers of glass pricked
my skin. I looked back to the opening and saw only a hand
clawing the air. I knew with certainty I was the only one
small enough to make that egress to safety.

The ship keeled again, both sideways and forward. With
every wave, it as if the entire vessel was being swallowed,
gulp by gulp, by the greedy mouth of sea. A shark-toothed
wind bit into my flesh and a cascade of waves swept me up
and water filled my throat. I gagged and coughed but my
throat was still closed. My lungs were filling faster than the
pigs bladders we blew up to use for sport. The ship groaned
and creaked and heaved once more. I was thumped against
the deck again, a lucky blow this time because finally I
choked and had a gasp of air.

But I had no hold.

I was spinning and sliding down towards the rest of them. Folks were piling atop each other, but still jostling, grabbing, clenched in a stranglehold between life and death.

Then? They were falling.

So numerous were they that I thought of dead flies on an old pane of glass in spring. Except dead flies cannot even buzz, let alone cry out with such ungodly shrieks and wails.

"John!" Strong arms had me by the waist.

"Dad?"

But it was Frith with a rope and he pointed to the mizzen.

"Climb and I'll join you as soon as I can!"

Rung by rung in the rigging I climbed. The tip of the mast was as spindly as the top part of a tree branch and I feared it would snap in the wind. I stopped mid way then tied a bowline knot, securing my ankles to the rigging. Back and forth I swayed and teetered. A boy in a swing.

Below me was the real pit of hell, filled with water not fire.

"John!"

"Ryan!"

He shinnied the ropes as nimble as ever, with a smile of relief and gratitude on his face. But then I saw it. I saw behind him a mountain of wave cresting higher and higher. There was a roar as it hit the deck and became a pummeling wall of water. Ryan held his hand up to me. I was beyond his reach, I was certain of it, and did not extend my hand to him. When the wave receded, Ryan was gone.

One after each after another, those below were vanishing before my eyes. I watched a man with his wife and baby for the longest time. He had hold of a bit of railing and was praying. His eyes locked mine just before the wave came that swept them under. Perhaps he said a prayer for me. I heard that baby crying, I did, for several godforsaken minutes longer.

Once again, time slowed down. The ship rolled over on its belly, gentle like, as if it were some old man merely trying to settle into a good night's sleep. I was then staring almost face down at the frenzy of waves below. I flapped about, like a rag in the wind. My fingers were just frozen nubs.

The vessel dipped and then I was flying outwards wondering why it was the moon had simply disappeared.

— WHICH WITCH? —

Hamamelis virginiana! Translation: witch hazel! Or maybe my grandmother was a chameleon. That's all there was to it, I decided. Just when I thought I was getting a handle on her, just as I was changing my feelings about her in light of Harv's great love and endless devotion to her, just as our mutual interest in the shipwreck was bonding us together in a loose kind of way, I was brought up short. Another side of her emerged. The Wacko Witch. My grandmother truly was a witch of sorts.

"Hurry up, now, get outta bed, my clients will be here by ten. Lazy Mary, will you get up," she began to sing. I covered my ears.

"And I can't have you clattering about the kitchen. I'll need quiet for concentrating."

She stood in the doorway of my bedroom, one hand on her hip as if she was about to go into an "I'm a little teapot" routine. Well, she *was* short and stout, like the song said. This particular morning she was dressed up by her standards—brown corduroy pants and a moss green sweater that matched her eyes. For once, she wasn't wearing that hat and her hair was brushed. It was a mop of gentle curls the colour of ashes from the end of a cigar.

"Have you got any lipstick?" she asked.

"Dad won't let me wear it yet," I said, blinking the sleep, as well as the surprise, out of my eyes. Carolina warned me people would think I was a tomboy because I didn't give a hoot about make-up. She insisted I put on lip gloss at school. Corporal Ray did not know.

But the Vinegar Witch wearing lipstick?

"Well, that still doesn't mean you don't have any in that bag of yours."

She looked at me all wide eyed. She'd been snooping!

I threw back the covers, glad I'd brought my flannel pyjamas and kept on my socks. The floor, even through my socks, felt colder than a skating rink.

"It's cranberry," I said.

"That'll do fine. My lips are dry, is all."

She fumbled in front of the mirror and smudged it on.

"Do this, Nana," I said, poking my finger in my mouth and smacking. "That way it won't rub off on your teeth."

"That right?" she said. "Well now." She did as I said and giggled. "Never been much into beautifying, you know," she said.

Like I hadn't noticed.

She handed me back the tube.

"No, keep it," I said. "I think I only ever wore it at Halloween."

"Thanks." She even managed a wobbly cranberry smile. She looked almost pretty. Now if only she'd do something about that chin hair.

"So, Nan, what's the occasion? Getting hitched to Harv today?"

"That's enough out of you now."

"And what do you mean, clients?"

I was back in bed with the covers up to my chin, shivering. She sat down on the foot of my bed. She started picking threads on the worn-out quilt. Then she looked around the room.

"Quite the decoration scheme you've got here." She got up and examined my clothesline of clippings and paint-swatch collages. "Lots of history and local colour."

"Ha ha. You're changing the subject," I said.

She sighed and sat back down. "Well, I don't get so much from my old age security cheque, and last winter the furnace had to be replaced and next year it'll be the roof, no doubt. So. Well, I've started this little business on the side, you see."

This was something my father didn't know about. He would have mentioned something like this.

"What sort of business?"

"Tea leaves."

"I beg your pardon?"

"I read tea leaves," she said with the same expression as a person might say "I sell real estate."

"You mean like a fortune teller or something? You read people's futures?"

"No! That's just Pugwash—I mean hogwash. Hocus-pocus. Those nitwits on TV, that's all a hoax. I grow my own herbs out back, as you know. Then I harvest them and pound them and brew up some tea and serve it in the sunroom and, well, they say I have the gift."

"The gift?"

"It's called tasseography, the reading of tea leaves. I interpret the symbols left at the bottom of the cup. You have to know what you're looking at. Then it's plain as day."

"Cool," I said. Not that I meant it. From geography to tasseography? Was it a sign of some old-age disease?

"Well, I don't how cool it is, but four clients once a week is one hundred bucks, and times that by four and that's four hundred extra dollars a month I've got. Not bad. Anyhow, you slept in this morning and I didn't want to bother you, but they'll be here in an hour."

"I'll go out for my run, then." I sighed as if this was a sacrifice.

"You don't have to stay away the whole time or anything like that. I just wanted the breakfast things over with."

"Okay."

She whistled on her way downstairs.

I peeked in the sunroom before my run. It was completely decked out. I couldn't believe my eyes.

"Wow! Nana!" I said.

"Well, I try my best but—"

"But nothing," I said. "It's beautiful!" And it was.

The old pine drop-leaf table had been pushed to the centre of the room, with five chairs around it. She'd covered it with a creamy white tablecloth embroidered with delicate blue and yellow pansies. It had been freshly ironed. A vase of her garden flowers, brown-eyed Susans and bright orange tiger lilies, made "an eye-catching centrepiece" my mother would say was to die for. On the buffet, her best china teapot and teacups were arranged on a tray, ready to serve.

"And what's that delicious smell?" I asked.

"Scones," she replied, "that I'll serve with Devonshire cream."

"No, it's another smell."

"Lemon balm, spearmint and rosemary and a few secret ingredients," she teased. "It's brewing in the kitchen now."

"Well, I think you could charge more, just for sitting in the room with this view," I said.

She gave me a hot scone for breakfast. Was it a peace offering? A truce? Where was the witch? Who was the which? Which witch was she this morning?

— PLAN B —

"Minikin!" Max was poking around down on the beach not far from Poplar Grove. I waved and slowed down.

"Come get a look at this!"

He was wearing what he always wore. I knew folks in East Boulder were mostly fishing folks without a lot of money, so I tried not to judge. "Judge not your friends by outward show, the feather floats high but the pearl lies low." It was one of Corporal Ray's favourite lectures to me. Besides, Max always smelled clean as the ocean air. And he looked good, anyhow. His sweatshirt was blue, faded by the sun and salt. It matched his eyes. He wore a pair of denim shorts frayed at the cuffs. His sneakers were orange canvas and rubber, scuffed on the toes. The sole of his right sneaker was torn. Sometimes, it made a flapping sound when he walked.

"What is it?" I panted. I hoped he thought the panting was just from my run.

"You tell me."

It was a ring. A green stone set in gold was wedged between two rocks.

"An emerald? From the wreck?"

He shrugged.

"Looks pretty old."

"Looks can be deceiving," he said. "Could have been anyone's, I guess. Take it—it's yours, Minikin."

I picked it up.

"Well, put it on!" he said.

I just stood with my mouth open like some kind of fool. "Where I come from, if you take a ring from a boy—"

"What?"

"It wouldn't be right," I mumbled.

He threw back his head and laughed. "Don't get excited. We're too young to get married . . . yet."

I turned Valentine Red. Romantic Red. Red-y or Not.

"Can't you just take it as a gift . . . from an old pal?"

"Sure." Pal. Old. "Thanks." The darn ring fit.

"How's the petition going?" Guess he needed a topic change too.

"It's not."

"Why not? Go door to door yet?"

"No. I've been training, and besides, it's useless. It's like Nana said. Nobody cares."

"Don't say that! There are still folks whose dead relatives helped in the rescue that night. They'd all care. And

I care. And my own mother and father would care."

"Well get them to sign, then. Three signatures so far. Harv's store is always filled with people. My name, Nana's and Harv's. Whoopdy-doo. Like I said, who cares?"

"Gravesaver! That's you! That's who!" He poked me in the ribs. "You've got to do something bigger than this petition idea, anyhow. Actions speak louder than words."

"I couldn't agree with you more. But what?"

"Look out!" He pointed ahead. The limousine was coming towards us.

"Hardly Whynot!" I whispered.

"Who?"

"Hardly. As in Whynot. Haven't you heard the rumour that he's renting Admiral Fullerton's place? If it's true, all I want is *his* signature!"

"Great! Then you'll have four on your petition."

"No, silly! An autograph—for my mother! She's a huge fan and she's been sort of down in the dumps, I guess you could say. What a surprise it would be. I mean ... Oh my ... Mississippi! What an idea! You said 'something big.' He's big. Major big. He's *huge*. What if I got him interested? He's even got money. Swimming pools of it, I've heard. The *Atlantic* left from Liverpool, his home town, come to think of it. There's a connection. Oh, I've got it! Get Hardly on this and we have ourselves a restored grave!"

I hugged him. Then I got overheated.

I rewound to Nana's. "Gimme Your Hand to Hold." The Ladybugs song blared into my head because as my arms shot out from my sides, the ring on my hand sparkled. *We're too young to get married . . . yet.*

So he was a flirt. A tease. Still, I wanted to hug him even tighter, not just hold his hand.

— THE CACKLEBERRY WOMEN —

Nana's "clients" were still in the sunroom. It was lunchtime, my brain was buzzing, and I had that lopsided feeling again. I was starving.

"Minn, that you?" Nana called out. I was trying to sneak a scone up to my room.

"We won't bite," someone said. Her voice was deeper than any trucker's fuelling up at Harv's.

I stuck my head in and immediately wished I hadn't. The four of them looked ready to pick at my bones, and I got that fluttery warning feeling in the pit of my belly.

"They want to meet you, Minn," said my grandmother. Her left eyebrow did that leapfrog hop it did sometimes. If I wasn't mistaken, the look she gave me was more an apology. And those eyebrows kept ahopping. Okay, so if I was reading the telegraph correctly she was also saying to me: "Humour them, puh-leeze, they're hopeless."

"Why would you want to meet me?" My tone was borderline rude.

"We've seen you out running these past weeks. We're renting the cottages up on Poplar Grove."

Her words were slurred. I realized with a bit of a shock that they had been knocking back some of Nana's blueberry wine.

"Yes, you're a speedy little devil. Good for you. But we've got a question," she continued. The woman was older than my mother, I think. Her neck was so long she made me think of a giraffe. "We're staying in the rental cottages up on Poplar Grove Hill," she said again.

"Oh, Sylvia, cut to the chase," wheezed another woman in tight leather pants.

"We saw you talking to the chauffeur," said the third woman. She was the one with the trucker's voice.

"Hardly's chauffeur," said the final woman. "At least that's what we think. One of the famous Ladybugs— before your time, dear—" they all cackled at this, "is renting Admiral Fullerton's mansion for the summer. Or so we've heard."

"Do you know if it's true?" asked Ms. Leather Pants.

"Can't tell you exactly if that's so, but I have my own suspicions as well." I saw the opportunity for some fun.

"What makes you think so? What did he say?"

"He asked me first if I lived in the area and wanted directions to the city because he had to make a trip to a music store for new guitar strings for his boss."

"Aha!"

My grandmother was nearly busting a gasket, trying to hide a smile behind her hand and peering into the teacups as if she was still seeing the future there, far below, in the bottom of the ocean.

"Oh, you're just our pulling our legs," said one of the women. "Aren't you?"

I shrugged. "Well, if I knew but was sworn to secrecy, I couldn't go telling what I knew, now, could I? Look, if you really want to know for sure who's living there, you should go find out for yourself."

"But there's No Trespassing signs all over the place."

"True," I said. "But there's a secret trail by the hedge of pear trees at the west edge of the property that'll lead up to the stone wall. There's a crack in the foundation and you can get close enough to spy on the house. My father took me there once. We just wanted to see the house. Anyhow, if I were you and lived that close, I'd be tempted to take some binoculars and go find out. Careful of the poison ivy, though."

"Well, your grandmother just told me I was going to meet someone rich and famous very soon," said Ms. Leather Pants. "It's got to be him!"

"I don't know, really I don't," I said and excused myself. Their cackles were getting on my nerves. Their blueberry-wine breath was gross. From my window I watched the Cackleberry Women stumble back up the road towards Poplar Grove Hill.

The tea leaves were still at the bottom of the cups as I rinsed them out.

"Nana, do you believe in this, really, that reading tea leaves can tell you things like you told them?"

She didn't answer at once. "It's not so important if I do really. I think it's more fun than anything. Just something my own mother did. It's the people who want to hear that there's good news ahead, or some excitement in their dull and boring lives, that needs to believe. Yes indeed. Belief can make a lot of things possible."

— NEW NEWS FROM HOME —

Every morning I tried to write in the journal Miss Armstrong-Blanchett had given me. And every morning I crossed out almost everything I wrote. Talk to the page? What was there to say?

The training diary was easier. How long I ran. Calculation of distance. Calf stretches or hamstring curls. Jumping jacks and sit-ups. Push-ups. How many sets. Weather conditions. Mostly it was cloudy. Still, it was stuff you could make sense of. Sometimes, I was just plain bored out of my mind. I pinned more and more of the articles about the shipwreck across my room. I tore out more swatches from my mother's paint fan deck and made a collage on my wall over the peeling wallpaper.

Rigbyisms yelled at me from every nook and cranny. *Get off your gluteus maximus! Just Begin!* He even phoned a few times.

"Minn?"

"Yeah?"

"How's it going?"

"Fine."

"Working hard?"

"Yeah."

"Good stuff. Doing your visualizations?"

"Trying to."

"Good stuff. Okay, bye."

A man of action and very few words. Except for those Rigbyisms. Truth was, my most creative visualization was my room. Nana called it a decorator's nightmare. I liked what I had done just fine. And to her credit, she did give me some back issues of her precious *National Geographics* I could cut pictures from and paste on the wall.

I kept rearranging my treasure drawer. I put down a soft piece of flannel I found in the rag pile under the bathroom sink. All the treasure I was finding along the shore was in there in a circle. I made a little bed for the skull in the centre.

I took it out often and cradled it on my chest as I lay in bed. There were cracks in the plaster in the ceiling. One afternoon I began to play the same game with the cracks as I did with clouds. A tulip opening. A giant bunny. The face of . . . a deer. There was . . . the phone ringing and Nana calling: "Minn, it's for you. Some fella!"

Max?

"Hello?" My voice was as casual as possible.

"How's my girl?" Corporal Ray!

"Oh. Dad."

"Whatever happened to 'Hey there Daddy-o!'"

"I'm not a child."

"Things not going so well?"

"No no, everything's fine. Tickety-boo."

"Running much?"

"The gold will be mine!"

"Atta girl!"

"Put Mum on?"

Silence. Clearing of throat.

"I can't. Your mother is . . . Your mother has . . . Your mother went out to see Aunt Ginny."

"In British Columbia? The other side of the country? I thought you two needed time alone."

"Sometimes a change is as good as a rest. Maybe she needs her sister right now." He didn't sound too convinced.

"Maybe I need my mother right now!" I hissed.

"Sisters can be good comfort for each other," he added.

"I wouldn't know, would I?" I slammed down the phone and ran to my room. The phone rang again. I heard Nana talking. I pounded my pillow.

So. My mother left my father and was all the way across the country. When was she coming back? Or maybe it wasn't a when question. Maybe it was an if. *Was* she coming back? Ever?

I crept across the room and put my ear to the door.

"Ray, she's homesick as anything. Why not come for a visit? I see. I see. Well, that's too bad then. But the girl's been working herself so hard. I don't know about this running business. Not natural. She'll have arthritis someday from this. Get her mother to send a postcard, for heaven's sake, at least."

That was enough. Nana Vinegar taking my side and feeling sorry for me. I was feeling sorry enough for myself.

I reached for more newspaper clippings and leafed through the stories of the disaster. I had pinking shears.

I paper-clipped more on my clothesline and added to the walls.

HUNDREDS OF DEAD BODIES
WASHED UP ALONG THE SHORE
RELATIVES ARE BEING NOTIFIED
OF THE DEAD AND MISSING

Maybe it's awful to admit, but it made me feel a bit better. I polished my skull and put her back in my treasure drawer. I plumped up my pillow. Then I reached for the box I'd shoved far away. The one that spooked me. The tiny cardboard coffin. I took a deep breath. I snapped off the criss-cross of red elastics and opened it.

I was wrong. I didn't find more bones.

I found a beating heart instead.

John Hindley's.

⤖ Jump and Hope ⤖

The ropes held me fast. A woman scaled the ropes below
me. Maryanna.

I watched as she stopped a few rungs over, steadied herself as best she could and then ripped her nightdress from
her ankles upwards. She fashioned ties out of the tatters
and bound herself to the mizzen.

Down below to our right, a mass of purplish seaweed
floated in a whirlpool of waves. The hide-and-seek moon
appeared then and everything was illuminated. Maryanna
screamed. It wasn't seaweed.

Bodies, floating together as if caught in a net, bobbed
back and forth. Dead. All of them.

Then, Maryanna started singing. Yes. She was *singing*.
By this time her hair was wrapped around the ropes,
frozen there like a tangle of snakes. A necklace sparkled
against her throat. A ring glittered on her finger. Her lips
were blue and soon the song was nothing more than a

rusty croaking. Whispers. Whispers. Whispers.

"John—stay awake! Miss Rayborn—keep the songs coming."

It was Frith, climbing up to us as he'd promised.

I drifted in and out for a spell , but when my hands let go and I flopped over backwards I came to. *Catch me catch me catch me can.*

"Dad?" I flapped about, a human sail.

"Rise up!" Frith shouted. "Get back in the mizzen."

But I had no will left to do his bidding. I closed my eyes for what I hoped would be eternity. A wave slapped me fierce and directly in my line of vision, my mother's cradle appeared, floating on top of the waves as if rocked by an invisible arm. I gathered all my strength to right myself then, using my leg muscles the way I did whenever I climbed up into my father's arms.

Maryanna was silent; her eyes wide open with that same startled look I'd seen on my brother's face. The ring still shone. Every few moments, its light circled my head, like a lighthouse beacon nudging me awake.

On a hump of rocks several hundred feet away, a straggle of men had made it to safety. I watched others try—hand over foot—to shinny the length of the lifeline they'd rigged from the remaining deck. As the hours passed, it was clear very few would be strong enough to make it there. And then, even then, some were washed away once they got there.

Eventually, light leaked through hairline cracks in the dark clouds.

"Hang on! They're coming!" Frith was alive. There was a boat, a small one, tossing about in the swell. "Jump when I tell you!"

I used my knife between my hands like a saw and tried to hack through my ropes. I fumbled and it was lost.

Five times the men in the boat tried to get in position beneath the mizzen rigging. Then I lost sight of it.

"Now!" Frith screamed. And I jumped. I put all my weight in the jump, leapt out into the air, feeling the rope whip out from my ankles. Just before I hit the water, I took a deep breath, all what was left in me.

— FACE TO FACE —

John Hindley's heart was pounding, on a brittle page of newsprint.

-Lone child survivor-

What followed was the description of how he'd been saved in the nick of time, fished out of the water after hours clinging to the ropes of the mizzenmast.

> The boy is twelve from what we can gather. And comes from Ashton-under-Lyne, England. He seems most unaffected by events. Although he lost both parents and a brother, Thomas, he had few words for us. The family was bound for New York City, where he has sisters. Already some in the community have offered to adopt him.

Then, on the next page, his picture. *A face. John Hindley.* Staring up at me from speckled newsprint. His eyes laser-beaming into mine. I recognized those eyes. Eyes filled with sorrow and secrets.

I placed his picture in my treasure drawer. Next to the baby's skull.

— OUT ON A LIMB —

I told Nana I was going out for a long run after supper.

"You're going to waste away to nothing burning all that food you just put into your belly so fast. There must be some kinda rule like when you can't go swimming for an hour after eating. But all right. Get yourself home before dark."

Dressed in a green sweatshirt and beige splash plants, the perfect camouflage and très chic athletic wear, Cinnamon Hotchkiss, girl sleuth, set out upon her mission.

My mission was clear to me. I had to see if Hardly Whynot was at the Fullerton mansion. John Hindley's picture made me more determined than ever to save the gravesite. I was trying to think big and get Hardly's name on the petition. And even better would be publicity from his name and some money from his wallet!

Nana's binoculars thumped against my chest as I jogged around the bend and out of sight. I'd convinced her I wanted to watch some birds! At night? But she bought it. Then, for the first time all summer, I turned into Poplar Grove Lane. The cottages were crowded together at the upper end of the lane that twisted and turned like a maze I had to guess my way through. Finally, I came to a fork in the road that branched off in three directions. I chose the middle road, winding my way through yet another puzzle of cottages until I reached a long stretch of woods behind a high cedar thicket. This was it, the boundary line for the Fullerton mansion.

A black iron gate aswirl with sailing ships marked the entrance to the estate. The gate was locked shut and the house was well hidden from view. A row of old-fashioned streetlights made it look like something from the last century. The lampposts were new, and mounted on each, I spotted surveillance cameras. I sprinted past, hoping I would be just a blur on the monitors. The theme song from *Mission: Impossible* played in my head.

Farther along the main road, the wrought-iron fences joined up with a high stone wall that snaked into the woods, past a grove of apple and pear trees. This was the place. I ducked off the main road and followed an overgrown trail that looped between the wall and the edge of a cliff overlooking the ocean. The trail was wide, but I hugged the stone wall and was tempted to crawl on my hands and knees. It was a long way down.

The wind was blowing something fierce and I didn't remember the trail being this snarled when I was here with Corporal Ray. After a bit, I spotted a section of the house. Inside a screened-in porch was a table made of twigs and wooden deck chairs painted pink and yellow. A hammock made of fishnet was suspended along the side of the porch. A telescope was mounted on a tripod. Perhaps Hardly Whynot had an interest in the stars.

The chauffeur was mowing the front lawn. Anchored at a wooden dock was an impressive outboard—more like a yacht—as well as a rowboat. A buoyed sailboat bobbed on the waves close by. Then I spotted *him*.

Sure enough, at the side of the boathouse, a man was hanging up life jackets and floating devices. Hardly! Or so I hoped. I lifted the binoculars and tried to focus, but he kept ducking out of view. I didn't know how I could position myself so I could get a good look. If I jumped up the wall, they'd spot me for sure. If I climbed through the crack in the wall to get closer, I'd be on their property. The No Trespassing signs said there was a thousand-dollar fine.

My only option, it seemed, was the tree above my head. Up I went, nimble as a squirrel, and out onto a branch. I was halfway along when I realized that the branch hung out over the edge of the cliff. I froze. Completely. Frothy waves eddied below me and made me dizzy. The water seemed half-solid—like a heaving floor of jade green marble. Then the weirdest feeling came over me. I felt like jumping.

Okay. Okay. Breathe. Breathe. Back up. Slowly slowly slowly.

"Come on! It's my turn! Gimme!"

I almost jumped out of my skin and slipped, just catching myself in time.

The Cackleberry Women! The four of them were on their hands and knees making their way to the crack in the wall. And laughing like fools. By the sound of them, I'd say they'd all been dipping into that blueberry wine again.

From out of nowhere, the biggest, meanest, blackest Doberman pinscher I've ever seen came tearing up the yard headed right towards them. If I hadn't been so scared myself, I would have fallen out of the tree laughing. The sight of those four, in their high heels and designer clothes, hightailing it out of there, falling and grabbing each other, was like watching one of those prize-winning home videos on TV.

But the dog stopped at the crack in the wall and barked up at me! It must have smelled the sweat rolling off my forehead.

The man from the boathouse shouted to Mafia man, who stopped mowing and headed straight towards me.

He stood for several seconds at the wall, looking around. He patted the dog and told it to be quiet.

"What you see out there, girl? A spy? Come on, Hannah, it's probably a fox."

He returned to his mowing, and I inched my way back to the tree trunk and slid down, grateful to be on firm ground again. I ran, all right. I just barely avoided running into a huge patch of poison ivy.

Hannah! It hit me. "Hey Hannah" was a famous Ladybugs song. Well, my mission had been successful after all. How much more evidence did I really need?

My brain was whirling faster for another reason, too. Up in that tree I'd spotted Elbow Island. From that height it looked like an arm, beckoning. There was a flash of orange through the trees. Max? Yes, it was. Rowing towards the island in a small dory.

I was more than curious. Maybe—he'd take me the next time?

Nana would never let me.

But if Hansel and Gretel could do it, so could I. Find some way to escape from the clutches of the old witch.

≈ Mind Fog ≈

The arms of a woman held me close. Her eyes were the soft brown of a doe's. The eyes of mercy.

"Drink," she whispered. The words tickled my ears like bits of fleece. She held a flask to my lips. The burn in my throat!

Next thing I knew there were other arms, a man's arms, picking me up, carrying me to warmth.

Hours slipped by, like clouds drifting over the face of the moon. I lapsed in and out of sleep and nightmare and woke up huddled on a bed wrapped in a quilt. Folks filed in and out, stopping for food and drink, for a shut-eye as the recovery of remains was under way.

In through the door limped a man. Dad!

"John, you made it, son." He reached out to me, grabbed both my hands and held his forehead to mine. I felt the bristle of his whiskers against my cheek and realized it was Frith, not my father.

"Our hero, the man who swam out to rescue us, is one Reverend William Ancient," he told me. "The minister in these parts, a sailor he was before called to be a saviour of souls. God knows I have never been a religious man and only God knows why we were spared and so many was not. I expect I have a debt to pay in this life now."

My folks were gone.

I understood this even before I found out no other children or married folks made it. The men stayed by the sides of their wives, it was said. It brought me some comfort picturing that. Paddy and Mary Hindley clinging to each other in their last hour as they had their whole lives.

I heard a scream then. My scream.

I had just remembered Thomas.

— HARBOUR OF HATE OVERFLOW —

"No. No. No. And furthermore, no. You are not taking the boat out."

"Nana! I'm really good. Dad even said. I'll wear a life jacket!"

"No!"

I did my stomp dance up the stairs and then slammed the door to my room.

"Oh you can have your little show of hysterics, missy, but it won't change my mind any."

"You sour old mountain goat," I muttered, not quite loud enough for her to hear.

There was my Rigbyism of the week, mocking me as I threw myself down on top of my covers.

Breathe. Breathe. Breathe. This is an exercise to help calm you and remind you that air really is the breath of life. Learning to be conscious of your breath and breathing techniques, becoming aware of your diaphragm and chest pushing oxygen throughout your body, is essential to an athlete. It can also help you achieve mental clarity. Try taking five deep breaths and be aware of your body as you do this. Gradually increase this conscious breathing time each day until you can do twenty breaths without getting dizzy.

I took a deep breath and held it until I couldn't any longer. If I hadn't I would have screamed.

We still weren't talking to each other when Harv came over for his nightly visit.

"I'd say I need a machete to cut the tension round this place tonight," he commented. "So what gives?"

"You're in love with a heartless woman," I said to him.

"Heartless, am I? Well, Harv, tell your royal highness here that heartless is better than spineless, which is exactly what I'd be if I gave in to her every whim and wish!"

"And what's that?" asked Harv.

"She wants me to let her go gadding about out on the water with some feller. She's twelve. He's fifteen!"

"Whoah? Who's this now? And why not bring him around?"

I ignored the question.

"Harv, help me out here. Talk some sense into her."

"Now, Minn, d'ya know how many years I've been

trying to get this woman to marry me? I'd have better luck at horse shoes than changing her mind once it's set."

Maybe she thought we were ganging up on her.

"And furthermore, it's not me making the rules anyhow," she sputtered. "Your father said your mother's death afraid of you going near the water."

So that was it. My loony mother and her crazy dream. "My mother!" I spit out. "My mother is a lunatic. You're gonna listen to her?"

"Don't you dare say any such a thing about your poor mother!"

Two splotches of red appeared on each cheek. Was she shocked at what I'd said? Well, well, just wait, I thought. There's a whole lot more you should know, old lady.

"Poor mother?" I scoffed. "She's off her rocker! Poor me's more like it! You weren't there last winter and all this spring, Nana! I was! All she did was stare into space, listen to old sad sobby Ladybug records, took to wearing black and beige. My mother, the rainbow goddess, wearing beige? That's normal? She never talked. I think she lost her tongue, not just that baby! She doesn't even know I'm alive any more—what difference would it make to her if I drowned out there?"

The words came spraying out like water from a burst fire hydrant. But I was on a roll. I filled in lots of holes in the information she thought she had about my family and then some.

"All I ate for months was macaroni and cheese—K.D. Golden bullets! At the end of the year, after she'd slept for months, she was still too tired to come to our sports banquet. Tired? What a joke. She's just gaga bonkers." I spiralled my finger by the side of my head. "Off her jee-zluz rocker, okay?"

Nana clomped across the room and shook me by the shoulders. "Stop it! Stop that this minute! Calm down!"

"Don't you touch me, you sour old vinegar witch!"

"Well, Flin Flon to you too!" she snapped back and gripped me tighter.

"Girls!" Harv was covering his ears.

I squirmed away and flew off the veranda. I ran and ran and ran long after it grew dark. Past Ludlow's, looping around Poplar Grove, on out to Boutillier's Point, and finally I found myself stumbling through the dark on the road to the gravesite.

I hesitated only a minute. I found the path and entered the woods.

— SPOOKED —

The moon was bright. Strange as it sounds, I found relief there among the tombstones. In fact, I realized I was more comfortable with the dead these days than the living. I sat down near the monument, put out my hand, traced the markings with my fingertips. Then I lay down on the ground and watched the stars. It made me think of Corporal Ray. Trying to trace the Big Dipper with his finger. I thought of my mother, holding up a paintbrush, some of the paint on her nose. "Voilà! Moonlight Mist!" I got a very sad throat. I had to swallow five times for it to go away.

There was a rustle in the grass. Footsteps.

I peered around the monument.

He looked as though he was playing some sort of weird leapfrog-over-the-dead game.

He hopped closer. I held my breath. Closer. When he was almost on top of me, I stood up.

"AHHHH!" I swear he jumped ten stories high. "What on earth are *you* doing here? You scared the poo— You spooked me but good!"

I couldn't stop laughing. I laughed so hard I snorted. How romantic.

His eyes twinkled. Even in the dark I could see that glint of fun.

"Why are you here?" he asked again. This time his voice was tender. He touched my face with his index finger. "You've been crying. Why?"

"I wasn't."

"You're not a very good liar."

"I found something the other day. Here." I reached into my pocket and unfolded John Hindley's photo. "It made it all so real, Max. Putting a face on things, you know? He lost his folks. His brother. It's their bones in this gravesite—if they haven't already been washed out to sea. Look, I want to go out to Elbow Island. I've got a plan. Well, an idea, anyhow. I was going ask you to come . . . but forget it . . . my Nana . . ."

Max squinted at the newsprint. After a while he said, "Minn, I'll do anything I can to help you."

"Really?"

"Cross my heart, hope to die, stick a needle in my eye."

Then he did it. He lowered his head. He brushed my forehead with his lips.

That spooked both of us. He cleared his throat.

"Want me to walk you back to the road?"

"No, I'm okay," I croaked out.

He cantered back into the darkness. Flap, flap, flap went his sneakers. Flutter, flutter went my heart.

But I should have gone with him. The cemetery was a graveyard after he left. A place for bones. I shivered. I searched the sky for stars. They had disappeared. I raced back through the tangle of woods, tripping and bumping into tree trunks. A haunted forest. Was it Dorothy from the *Wizard of Oz* who wrestled with monster trees that came to life? I couldn't remember. I kept seeing a newspaper headline: "Child Found Dead in Tangled Woods."

Back on the main road, I picked up my pace. There was a set of headlights behind me. When I slowed down to a walk, it felt as if my lungs would pop. I shook like a jellyfish blob as the car approached and then cruised beside me. For one brave second, I considered striking off into the woods again. Thoughts of bears and child-snatching trees made me change my mind.

The car stopped. A door opened.

"Get in."

— NOT SO JOLLY —

It was a truck, not a car. It was Harv, not a killer.

"You look like something the cat drug in," he said.

I started to laugh, but the choked sounds quickly turned to tears.

"Let it out, sweetheart," he said softly. Then he passed me a rough-torn piece of paper towel, dirty with grease. "Blow," he said. "And cry till your heart's stopped aching."

"I can't," I confessed. "I c-c-can't. You don't understand . . . Did you ever have the feeling, Harv, that if you really let it out, like really felt what was inside so deep you didn't even know what it was that was hurting so bad, that you'd maybe never stop crying? Did you ever feel like that?"

He didn't answer right away.

"Honey," he said finally, "I'm an old man. I fought in the Korean War. I think I've known exactly how you feel most of my life."

"I never knew that, Harv—that you were in the war."

I thought of all those Remembrance Day parades where I watched Corporal Ray. He'd never been in any war, of course. He was just there to be a handsome Mountie, paying respect. All those old men were the real deal, though. Air force, marines, combat soldiers marching by with medals thwacking their chests and funny little berets on their heads. I always thought they looked so old and tired. But proud, too. They always gave me a sad throat. Harv didn't seem to be like them at all.

"I don't talk about it often," he continued.

Try as I might, I couldn't picture Harv as a young man with a gun, fierce-like, like you had to be in a war. I just couldn't.

"Did you ever *kill* anybody?" I asked before I thought about what I was asking. And I wanted to take it back before he answered.

Sitting there in the truck, with only the dash lights reflecting on that face of his—so wrinkled at this moment it looked like a design of tartan plaid—Harv Jollymore did what my father had once. He cried. Only differently. One lonely teardrop fell from his right eye, dripped down his face and off his jaw. Guess that was his answer.

He cleared his throat, spit out the window—gross!—and turned on the radio. I was still sorting all this out. Harv, the gentle giant he was, had seen things and done things I guessed he lived with and would rather forget.

My world seemed safe, suddenly, and I was embarrassed. I felt like a spoiled kid who hadn't got her way. I'd heard Nana tell him that the other night. "She's just spoiled rotten like so many kids when they're *the only child.*" Rub it in, witch.

The man on the radio said that winds were picking up. The coast guard issued a small-craft warning for the following day. Looked like no one would be heading out for Elbow Island any time soon. So much energy I'd wasted. All for nothing.

Nana acted as if nothing had happened when I returned. She brought me in a cup of tea while I was still reading.

"Special blend," she said. "Calms the nerves."

"You're what's getting on my nerves," I blurted.

"Here are some recent issues of *National Geographic.* Fascinating reading."

"Not to me."

She sighed. "Thought reading about the world might help get you out of yourself."

What on earth did *that* mean?

Who knows what she mixed in that potion of hers. I slept a dreamless sleep.

— BUBBLE BURSTING —

The next morning I woke up and touched my forehead.
Max and that kiss.

But mostly, I was excited about his promise to help
me save the grave. I hummed as I got out of bed. I was
in an unfamiliar bubble of happiness.

The thing about bubbles is they burst.

First off, Nana was wide-awake and perkier than
cayenne pepper.

"Guess what? Guess what? Guess what?"

"I give."

"Here!" It was a postcard from my mother. "I didn't
read it, though, letters are personal." Right. Then she
wagged a finger at the picture. "This is Tofino, on
Vancouver Island. Bee-you-tee-ful, eh?"

I took it to my room. My mother had printed teeny
tiny. In purple ink.

Dear Minn:

Auntie Ginny is treating me like royalty. B.C. is breathtakingly beautiful. I took a ferry ride from Horseshoe Bay to Vancouver Island. I soaked in a hot tub outside. I saw sea lions sunbathing on rocks. They bark! I met a family who have a pet seal. It visits them every morning at their dock. Her name is Lucille. Get it? Loo-Seal! Someday, Aunt Ginny wants you to visit. Wouldn't that be great?

Love,

Mom

Not "Love you more than all the stars in the universe." Not "I miss you over the top over the world and beyond Pluto." Not even "I miss you more than I missed the bus." Just, "Love." I wanted details. Like, was she coming back.

Aunt Ginny was not a real person to me. I'd only seen her in photos and knew her from phone calls. Aunt Ginny in B.C. When I was little this confused me. I pictured her living in the alphabet until I learned about abbreviations. There was no return address on the postcard. Thinking of my mother being out there with her sister instead of back home with her daughter made me furious. And what about Corporal Ray? He was drowning his sorrows in work. When I pictured him trying to yodel, nothing but the sound of his crying came back to me. I tore the stupid postcard up. I tore out all the yellows in her fan deck. Buttercup? Crushed. Sunflower? Smush. Morning Sun? In the garbage.

Another dent in my bubble: Hardly Whynot was being interviewed on TV. He was on tour in Russia. This meant, of course, he was not the man at the Fullerton mansion. So trying to get his help restoring the grave, or his autograph, was useless. I could just forget about sparking his interest or getting his money for the gravesite—unless he was going to take a private jet here right after the tour ended.

Who was I kidding? Even I couldn't find a scrap of imaginary hope to hang on to. Some little bubble to hide inside when everything is a disaster. I mean, not going your way.

Max didn't keep his word. I looked for him all day. I ran two entire extra sets of my regular route around Boulder Basin. No luck.

At the end of the day, my legs were so tired I wanted to cry. I studied John's photo again. *Do something*, I imagined him saying. "I will, I promise," I whispered. His eyes smiled at me. Or maybe it was just shadows playing tricks.

— HERRING CHOKERS —

"So what exactly is a herring choker, Harv?"

Harv was lighting his pipe. He and Nana had just informed me that the Herring Choker Picnic and Folk Festival was happening Saturday.

"Some think the word originally meant the one who deboned the fish before selling it, but over time, it was used more to describe a fisherman and then sometimes a certain kind of person. An unsavoury character, you might say. A scoundrel. You know, like we'd say, 'That Stubby McIsaac, what a herring choker he is, all right!'"

"Stubby!" I giggled. "How on earth would anyone get a name like that?"

"Take a gander," puffed Harv.

"Was he short and stubby?"

"No. Tall and thin, matter of fact."

"Did he smoke stubs of cigarettes?"

"He smoked the whole thing—no filtered kind."

"Did he have a stubble of whiskers?"

"Full beard."

"I know! He was stubborn! Stubby's short for stubborn?"

Nana chimed in, "Maybe that should be your new name!"

"Ha! Ha!" I said, not even looking in her direction.

Harv shook his head at us.

"Girls, girls! What am I going to do with you? Would it hurt you two to be civil to each other for a minute? Guess you're too much alike."

Nana laughed at this. Snorted, rather, pig-like. I was too insulted to speak. I knew Harv did not mean to hurt my feelings.

"C'mon, Harv, I give. Why would a man be called Stubby?"

"Stubby's another name for a low-necked bottle of beer or a bottle that holds other spirits. Stubby was our local bootlegger after he took over a thriving business from his uncle Gordie. Leastways he was until he got spooked out on Elbow Island one night and changed into a God-fearing man and ran a scrap metal business instead."

My ears quivered. *Elbow Island.*

"What happened?"

"The story's never really come out, but according to the Boulder Basin Gospel of Gossip at the time, he rowed out one night to Elbow Island, to where he kept one of his stills. No one knows what happened 'cept a storm came up and he spent the night, came home and went directly to Reverend Hardy's and asked to be rebaptized. They had a special ceremony that very Sunday, and Stubby never touched a drop again. Some think he had some sort of encounter with spirits drowned out there in the shipwreck."

"Are there ghosts out there, Harv? Even Nana thinks there are."

"Do not!" she snapped. Not very convincingly.

"Do too!" I said.

"Don't get him going with those ghost stories of Elbow Island." Nana shook her head in warning. "He's the one who got me half-believing."

"She should know some local history, Ida," said Harv as he relit his pipe.

"Harv, it's hogwash. Well, most of it anyhow." She started scraping furiously at dirt underneath her fingernail.

"Minn, my very own father said it was so. He spent one April the first out there. He was just a kid, and he took a dare. If he could spend the anniversary of the wreck of the *Atlantic* out there and survive, his buddies were going to pay him some cash. Even then, there were stories of ghosts out there. It's not such a long row on a calm night. Ten, maybe twelve minutes if you leave from Boutillier's Point. Anyhow, he got there and started scouting around for a place to set up camp. He heard footsteps. He stopped. The footsteps stopped. He shrugged it off and kept going. Heard footsteps again. He stopped. The footsteps stopped. He was too scared to look around, he said. Tried to tell himself it was the wind, or his mind playing games. So he went on like this for at least half an hour, getting more and more spooked with each passing minute. Finally he stopped, and this time—the footsteps kept coming. Closer and closer and closer. He almost ran screaming over the cliff, but he held his ground. And then—"

"Harv!" Nana was shrill.

"What happened?" I shrieked. My heart was bouncing around like a tennis ball.

"From out of the mist right up alongside of him, someone brushed right by. A man carrying his head beneath his arm. A headless man, he said. 'I swear on my life,' my dear old dad used to say, 'he passed me by and kept on going, fading back into that mist.'"

"Your father *saw* that? Really? Harv! No way."

"He swore up and down and used to make my mother so mad when he'd tell it. My father wasn't much of a joker or tease, so we kids all believed him."

Nana cleared her throat. "Pugwash!"

"Harv, do you think that's what happened to Stubby McIsaac? He saw the headless man?"

"All I know is he sure enough was a changed man. Still reads his Bible every day, I hear."

"He's still alive?" My heart did a flutter kick.

"Yep. Old, though. Been living up in the Sunnyvale Nursing Home for years now."

"So how about it, Minn," Nana said, "will you be coming to the picnic with us on Sayrday?"

"If by Sayrday, you mean Saturday," I mocked, "I'll have to think about it."

"Well, no flies off my back if you don't. I was thinking you could ask your beau."

"My beau? As if."

"Well, you might have fun enough, all the same," said Harv.

"I'll think about it, Harv. How about some reciting?"

"Tuckered out now, I'm afraid. Ida, it's your turn."

"*The Cremation of Sam McGee*, maybe, since we're on such a morbid topic."

I shrugged. She began. It made me think of Corporal Ray. It was his favourite. Guess he'd learned it from Nana.

As her voice droned on, I thought of Harv's father and especially of Stubby McIsaac. What did he know that could help me? I wasn't sure, but something told me to follow that funny little flutter kick my heart did a few moments ago.

— STUBBY —

Sunnyvale Nursing Home is just across the road from St. John the Baptist Anglican Church. It was Nana's church and we'd gone every Sunday since I'd been in Boulder Basin.

"There's no point in kicking up a fuss over going," she'd warned me the first Sunday. "It's important to have a spiritual community. For now, you're here in this community, maybe against your own wishes, but you'll be coming with me. You can pray for the health of your mother." If only she knew how I'd prayed—all last winter—and a fat lot of good that did.

Anyhow, I enjoyed the singing. Well, most folks' singing, that is. Nana knew most of the hymns by heart and sang them full blast off key. It was almost as bad as Corporal Ray's yodelling. I spent most of the service staring at the stained-glass windows and out the side door, which was propped open with a broom handle.

Even then, the church was always stuffy and smelled of candles and lemon oil. Through the door, I could see right across the street to the nursing home. Looked to me like those old folks spent the Sabbath having wheel-chair races up and down the sidewalk.

"I've come to visit Stubby McIsaac," I announced with as much confidence as I could to the woman behind the desk.

"Relative?" she asked, and then looked at me hard. "Why no, you're not!"

My mouth twitched but I held my smile in place.

"You've got to be Ida Hennigar's granddaughter. I'd know you anywhere—you're the spitting image of her." She beamed at me.

I rubbed my chin to see if there was hair growing there I hadn't noticed before.

"I used to date your father in high school," she said.

My eyes must have shown my surprise.

"A regular dream boat, he was!" she sighed, then caught herself. "Stubby will be thrilled to have a young visitor. Those grandkids of his hardly ever get in here to see him. Come this way. He's right over here.

"STUBBY! SOMEONE TO SEE YOU, DEAR!" She sounded like she was talking through a megaphone.

"EH?" he yelled back, cupping his ear.

His face was so shrivelled he reminded me of those little dolls people make out of shrivelled-up apples.

"A GIRL TO SEE YOU!"

"THAT SO?" he said, eyeing me up and down. The woman patted me on the shoulder and left.

"WHO IS YOU, YOUNG LADY? ONE OF MY GRANDCHILDREN?"

"MY NAME'S CINNAMON HOTCHKISS," I yelled.

"DID YOU SAY CINNAMON? THAT'S A FUNNY NAME!" Like he should talk. "CINNA-MON LIKE THE SPICE?"

I nodded.

"AND HOTCHKISS?"

I nodded again. This was going to be painful. Big mistake coming here.

"RELATED TO BURNS HOTCHKISS?"

I bobbed my head up and down like a yo-yo. He was a great-uncle or something.

Stubby McIsaac touched one of his ears and then the other. "There now, speak up, but you don't have to yell."

The old devil! He'd had his hearing aid off the whole time!

"So what brings you here?" he said.

There wasn't time to beat around the bush. This place smelled like cat pee and blue cheese. I wanted out as fast as I could. In the corner, a woman with no hair was sitting rocking a doll and singing to it. Her scalp was the same pink as the doll.

"Lullaby and good night with roses delight," she wailed and then just sang, "Lo lo lo lo lo lo lo lo lo lo lo."

I swallowed. "I heard a story," I said. "About you."

"Oh Lord in heaven, dear," he wheezed, "don't believe half of what you hear around these parts!"

"I am doing some, um, independent research on the SS *Atlantic*," I told him. I heard Nana telling Harv one night her *independent research* on herbs was coming along fine.

Stubby's eyes widened, then narrowed into slits. "I see."

"I need to know what happened the night you went out to Elbow Island. I heard it changed your life."

"For the better," he agreed, not once taking his eyes off my face. "But I've not told a soul the truth all these years. Why should I tell you now?"

"Because," I hesitated and then went for it. "Because, Mr. McIsaac, I would like to help save the gravesite."

He coughed. He smiled—a sad sort of smile. As though he felt sorry for me. "Found some bones, didn't you."

I nodded.

"I know all about it. You find the bones and then you're pulled into it. You find out what you can, right? I didn't read much but I did lots of askin'. You try to not think on it too much. But it's always there, isn't it. The bones speak. 'Who am I? Come find out.'"

"You do know."

"I do. And is it true what I've heard? The grave is almost washed back out to sea?"

"There's not much time left to save it," I said.

"Well, finally, a person with a good enough reason to tell my story to. Maybe."

"Please, I know it was a long time ago but . . ."

He slapped his thigh and chuckled. "Honey, I might not remember where I put my teeth last night but I'll 'member what happened that night until the day I die, which isn't so very far down the road, I suppose. Yes, well, maybe I should tell someone. Someone who might believe."

I smiled like a prize student who'd just got the right answer.

"How brave are ya?" he asked.

"Why?"

"It's not a tale for the faint of heart."

"I can take it."

"Why don't you wheel me out front and park me under that tree? It stinks in this place!"

— STUBBY'S VISION —

As soon as I settled on a bench across from him, Stubby nodded off to sleep. Great, I thought. But with his eyes still shut he mumbled, "I'm just gathering my thoughts. Clearing the cobwebs. The memories are sharp, but sometimes I lose the words."

As I waited for him to find them again, I thought about a lost and found for words that went missing. If I had that box full of lost words, I'd give it to the poor old man. Imagine seeing pictures in your head and searching for the words. Is being that old like always doing a crossword puzzle? My mother, in the good old days, coloured the world with her words. Perky Paprika! Fiddlehead Green! Vampire Vermillion. No, she'd never been at a loss for words—until she'd slipped into that silent place where words dribbled instead of gushed from her mouth.

The church bells began to ring. Like a signal, when

the last chime drifted out to sea, Stubby finally cleared his throat and started in.

"It was fine enough weather when I headed out that evening. I'd had a hard day and thought I'd make an overnight of it—something I'd always been meaning to do but never had. Thank God I had a few supplies, 'cause I no sooner anchored my boat than the wind kicked up something fierce. Then again, you know what they say about the weather round here. If you don't like it, wait five minutes, it's bound to change. She changes in a blink. We all know this.

"How old are you?" he asked suddenly.

"Twelve," I said.

"Well, then, I suppose I can tell you a bit more honestly. The thing of it is, my dear, I was three sheets to the wind that night."

"Pardon me?"

"Skunk drunk in the first place. I went out to Elbow Island that night to dip into my own supply. Can't really remember for the life of me now how that felt, to be that thirsty, but to one who's got the disease, well, you'd do most anything to get more when you haven't had enough. So there I was stumbling around on those slippery rocks, talking to myself and trying to make my way towards the still. That's when the rain started up. And I mean rain. Pour-down rain like the folks up yonder had turned on shower taps full blast. And the howl! The wind that night was like a chorus of voices, human voices rising and falling, you know the sound, a kind of Eou! Eou! Eou! sound. High then low then circling your head. Eou! Eou! Eou!"

He was shouting like a crazy man. A woman passing by on the sidewalk looked over at us in alarm and then hurried across the street.

Stubby took a breath and continued. "Hurricane, I started to think. Maybe some leftover tropical storm had made it all the way up the coast from Florida. I was soaked through to the bone in no time. I headed for a grove of trees mid-island where I knew the old Clancy cabin used to be. Sure enough, not that much of it was left, but I found it. I was happier than a pig in— Excuse me, my old words come back with memory, I guess. But I was feeling no pain. See, I'd found my refreshment along the way. So there I was. Had a sleeping bag, my drink and matches for a fire I always kept inside a leather pouch around my belt loop. I tore up some floorboards for kindling, snapped them with my boots and figured I'd be dried out—well, in one sense—in no time." He stopped and gulped some air. "I kneels down to light my fire and when I turned around and saw . . ."

His eyes were misty.

I waited.

"Where was I?"

"You said you saw . . . ?"

"Her. There she was."

"Who?"

"Honey, as real as you are to me now, I was looking into the face of the prettiest woman I ever saw in my life. What a sight for my sore eyes. Merciful Jesus, I thought to myself, I am truly blessed this night! I reached out to take her hand. I wanted to kiss it like a gentleman. But then . . ." He shook his head, scrubbed at his face with his hand, pulling his wrinkles down as he did. For a second, I saw him as a younger man.

"Then, she changed in front of my eyes into—into a corpse. Her eyes bulged out, almost popped out of her skull, and her lips were purple and her necklace kept shining in my face until I was blinded and fell to my knees. I felt it was the She-devil, a demon.

"'Lord have mercy!' I screamed.

"'Stubby McIsaac,' said an angelic voice. 'Look at me.'

"But I knew it was a trick.

"'Look at me!' she repeated.

"The cabin grew colder than death itself. I peeked out between my fingers like this."

He showed me. It was the way my mother watched scary parts in movies, through what she called a real handmade mask. I was gripping the edge of the bench, I noticed, and my legs muscles were tensed up, my palms sweating.

"And what did I see? She was the sweet young woman

again. 'Who are you?' I sputtered out. 'What do you want from me?' I asks her.

"'My name is Maryanna Rayborn. I died on the mizzen rigging in the wreck of the SS *Atlantic*. I am also the Woman of Whispers,' she whispered. 'I am the holder of all secrets and burdens you cannot whisper to any living soul. Not even yourself. I want your secrets, Stubby, and your burdens. Speak to me,' she said kindly.

"'And if I don't?'

"Again the dead woman rose up before me.

"'All right, all right!' I screamed. Hell, heck, I had enough secrets and burdens and some downright confessions to last me a lifetime." He blew through his mouth with a shudder of his lips, just like a horse does. "Are you religious, Cinnamon?"

"I'm not sure what I believe," I murmured, hoping my answer was okay. I was afraid he wouldn't go on with me telling the bald truth like that.

"That's fine, you can always believe in belief until you figure that out. Having faith is even better than having religion. Well, anyhow, I never knew what hit me. See, I was never much of a talker until that night, but I talked until the sun came up. Like she said, told her things I'd never told myself. And she did the strangest thing. When I was through, she waved her arms, and in through the door of that cabin, clouds drifted in. She whispered to them and waved her arms again. And then up blew this wind and the clouds swirled above my head and disappeared. 'Your heart can rest, Stubby. Your wounds are healed and burdens dissolved. Go forth in peace.'

"I cried like some baby and fell asleep. When I woke up, I made a promise to myself. That I'd never touch spirits again. The way I figured it, the spirits had summoned the spirits, if you get my drift. I never ever wanted to see that vision again—a face twisted in a mask of death." He stopped talking.

"How did she leave?" I asked.

"She just followed the clouds out the door like the gracious lady she was.

"Anyhow, I rowed, tunderation, I rowed back to the basin and went straight to Reverend Hardy's and asked to be born again in God's family. So there. The end."

"And you never told anyone?"

"Well, I did tell Hardy that day and my good wife who had prayed every night of our married life I'd mend my ways."

"And they believed you?"

"They believed it was the hallucinations of a drunken man. But I know better."

"How can you be sure?" I said.

"Because she gave me a name. A hallucination won't do that."

"Oh."

"See, I looked over the passenger list once. After my encounter. There was her name plain as the nose on your sweet little face."

"There *was* a woman who froze on the rigging out there. I remember reading that. But it didn't give her name."

"I'm just telling you what happened to me. So what will you do with this so-called independent research of yours?"

"I want to save the grave, Mr. McIsaac," I repeated.

"Isn't that a coincidence! There was a girl here before— Oh, that's you, isn't it!" he snorted.

Old people can smell really, really sour. Worse than vinegar.

"So what's your plan? How are you going to save it?"

"I don't know exactly. I've got a petition going. But I think I need to cause a stir somehow. Raise money."

"I have a hundred dollars to get you started," he said.

"No, no, I couldn't!"

"Oh yes you could!" He reached into his right slipper and pulled out a wad of bills. He winked at me. "They don't know I've got this." Then he peeled off a hundred. "Please," he said. "It'll make me feel real good."

I took it and tucked it into my jeans. It felt heavy as a rock.

"Go start yer stirring! Godblessnow. And if you find your way to Elbow Island, say hello to that beautiful woman for me, eh?"

"I've been thinking about it."

"Of course you have. Bones speak, like I said. And the arm that is Elbow Island beckons."

"I don't know how I'd get there. And it sounds dangerous."

"It is not for the faint of heart. If there's a will, there's always a way. And for those that dare, the rewards outweigh the danger. Trust me."

He began to wheel himself back to the front door.

"Did you ... um ... Did you see the headless man?"

"No. But Ace Jollymore did. Now, honey, I'm tired right out from so much talking. Talking takes breath and I don't have so many breaths left in me."

"Thank you, sir."

"Stubby," he said. "You can call me Stubby."

No, I thought, I really couldn't. Leastways, not with a straight face.

I shuffled home, hardly noticing where I was going. Trust him? Believe his story? He had been skunk drunk, after all. And yet? If an old lady could sit and rock and sing to a doll thinking it was a real baby, maybe a person could imagine just about anything. O.I.! O.I.!

— PICNICS —

The day of the Herring Choker Picnic and Folk Festival started early. Five thirty, to be exact.

"A picture-perfect day!" squealed Nana as she opened the curtains and let the sun flood in.

"Up and at 'em. Lazy Mary, will you get up, will you get up, will you get up. Lazy Mary, will you get up, will you get up this mooooorning?" she sang.

"All right, just please don't sing!" I protested.

"Rise and shine and give God your glory glory," she crooned in reply.

"Nana!"

"Good morning, good morning, good morning to you! Oh, we're all in our places with sunshiny faces! Oh, this is the way to start a new day!"

"How many wake-up songs do you know?"

"We rise again, in the faces of our children—"

"I'm up, okay!"

236

She was already halfway downstairs. "I'll need a hand loading the truck!"

I took a second to look out the window. She was right about the day. An endless blue sky. "Holland Blue." I heard my mother's voice so distinctly I spun around thinking she was in the room with me.

After breakfast, Harv and Nana headed for the fairgrounds to start setting up for the picnic.

There were training drills from me to tackle, but goofing off sounded like a better idea. I had a nice long soak in the claw-foot tub in Nana's room with lavender bubbles up to my neck. When my skin puckered up and started to peel, I drained the tub. My hair wasn't quite dry when the doorbell rang.

"Want me to walk you over?" Max asked. "I can't stay, of course."

"Of course."

The limo passed us. The chauffeur did his usual salute thing.

"What if I said I was going to Elbow Island?"

"How?"

"The boat."

"It's dangerous, and your grandmother—"

"I know. I've decided my grandmother doesn't need to know . . . And you'd be with me."

"At night?"

I nodded.

"I dunno," he said, but his voice cracked. His whole body, not just his face, started twitching. "But why?"

So I told him my plan. I had already taken the money Stubby had given me and spent some of it for materials to make an oversized dummy.

"What I want to do is use her as a decoy, you see," I explained. "Plant her out there on Elbow Island with a sign saying Save the Grave!"

"And then?"

"I'll call the coast guard and say someone's stranded out there. Then the media. Imagine the attention it will get if the media gets all fired up about it!"

"I'm pretty sure that would be illegal. You could get in all kinds of trouble."

"They won't have to know who did it. Are you in?"

"I'm not sure."

"Please!"

"No . . . it just wouldn't be right, like the boy who cried wolf."

"But it would work! Don't you care about the grave?"

He looked off towards the ocean. Then he sighed. "Okay. When do you want to go?"

By the time we arrived at the fairgrounds, the whole place was hopping. And when I turned around to say bye, Max was gone!

Folks were already sitting in front of the stage in fold-out lawn chairs and on blankets. Kids were running around with painted faces. I stopped and watched for a while at the booth. A woman with a crew cut of white hair and a wide smile painted everything from rainbows to kitten whiskers on kids' cheeks. She looked like she was having a ball and talked to each child softly as she painted. Her silver heart-shaped earrings sparkled in the sun. She was an older version of my mother. Maybe it was the paint connection. She spotted me at the fringe of the crowd.

"You're never too old to have your face painted," she said. I smiled. "So what's your fancy?"

"A heart," I said. "On my forehead."

"Well, I have to say I like hearts myself."

"I collect heart-shaped rocks," I told her. "They're all crooked ones, but it's cool looking for the perfect one."

"Maybe the crooked ones are perfect too," said the woman through pursed lips.

Slowly she drew the outline of a heart in the centre of my forehead.

"You want red?"

I shook my head. "How about that blue?"

She hesitated. "A blue heart means a sad heart," she whispered.

I pointed back to the blue. She held my eyes with hers.

"Okay," she said and began to fill in the paint with feathery strokes. It tickled. "Maybe it will change to white soon," she said. "A pure heart, dear girl, I think that's more you." I could have hugged her. If only she knew.

I paid her and set off towards the stage area.

The musicians were now going non-stop. I found a place nice and close to the front and settled on the grass. Two young women with flowing hair and velvety gowns began to play harp. It was magical. Next up was a three-man band.

"They sound good enough, but really, what's with the hair and those outfits?"

Nana stood behind me, arms folded. She smelled like onions. Guess she was still chopping and cutting.

"Here's a bit of money for a snack," she said, holding out a five-dollar bill.

"Thanks, Nana," I said. "I've got money."

"I know that. It's a gift. Can you take it, for heaven's sake?"

"Thanks," I said. I knew it was a lot of money for her.

Harv walked towards us, towering above the crowd.

"Stay here, Ida, for a sec," he said. "I know the next singer. She's a friend of my Molly's."

"That right?"

"Got her own CD and everything. Born and bred right here in Nova Scotia."

The woman's guitar was slung over her shoulder, suspended by a bright woven strap—happy colours, I thought. Someone adjusted her microphone as she tuned her guitar.

"Test, test," she said. "How you all doing today?" There were probably a good five hundred of us by this time.

"Great!" everyone shouted back at her.

"My name's Laura Smith and I'm glad to be here and right off I'm starting with a special request. Is Ida Hennigar here?"

"Lord God save my soul!" exclaimed Nana.

"Here!" I shouted and stood up, pointing at Nana. Everyone stared. I sat down fast.

"Ida, hello!" said the singer.

My grandmother was the colour of a raspberry and she smiled feebly, giving a little wave towards the stage.

"This one's for you 'cause I understand it's one of your favourites. Sent to you with love by that big strapping good-looking fella beside you. It's your birthday tomorrow, right?"

I'd forgotten! Dad had even pencilled it in my calendar.

"So first, before we get to the song, what do we need to do?"

Five hundred voices sang "Happy Birthday" to Nana. And clapped.

"Yes," said Laura Smith, "my note here tells me you'll be forty-five! You look too young for forty-five!"

Nana swiped Harv playfully on the arm and everyone roared.

"Anyhow, Ida, now here's your gift. I hope you like the way I sing it, ma'am."

And she started. "My Bonny Lies Over the Ocean." Never in my life have I heard it sung like that. Not a person so much as coughed. I can't describe this woman's voice. There was just so much inside it—like every sad and happy thought I ever thought. If I could bottle those up and pour them out like some golden liquid sound, that would be her voice. Soft and strong. Love and loss. Pain and joy. "Bring back, bring back, bring back my bonny to me," she crooned.

As she did, I swear I saw John Hindley. He mingled in the crowd, looking over the tops of people's heads, those laser-beam eyes of his zapping right into mine. Bring them back, he seemed to be saying, bring them back to me. A woman stood up and blocked my view. When she sat down again, he was gone. O.I.! O.I.!

Harv had his arm around Nana by the time the song was through. I turned to give her a smile and had to look away.

Her shoulders were heaving and she was choking back tears something fierce. Don't know why, but never once before had I imagined my Nana had tears inside her.

There was a silence when the song was over and then thunderous clapping, whistles, shouts. In that silence before it started, I felt how a whole crowd of people could feel like one. That's what Laura Smith did to us.

"Ida," she continued, "I also understand you like a good jig. So, folks, all of you up, and here's something a little more upbeat. Dance, everyone, come on!"

There we were tapping, swinging, clapping. Even me. After that, Harv and Nana went back to their meal preparations, and the woman who painted faces got up and sang. Some folks have so many talents. I felt her singing right to me.

In line at supper, I ran into the Cackleberries. Two of them were covered head to toe with poison ivy rashes. I turned away so I wouldn't laugh in their faces.

"What's this dish?" one of them asked Nana.

"Why that, it's jellyfish cream salad," Nana beamed. The poor woman turned white.

It was past midnight when we got home. Nana let me make her some mint tea. I couldn't believe she actually let me touch her herbs! But she was fast asleep on the sofa when I brought it to her. I covered her with a quilt and turned off the light. I went to my bedroom and changed into my pyjamas, but I couldn't sleep. I polished the baby's skull. I liked to make it warm.

I got out my journal. "Good Day. Good music. Good people."

For a brief second at the picnic, after hearing the music, I did what Stubby told me to do. For a second there, I believed in belief.

I think that's what Coach Rigby was getting at with all his Rigbyism and creative visualization exercises. If you believed it enough, you could do it. Maybe that's what Corporal Ray was doing too. If he believed my mother would get better, she would. If I believed in saving the gravesite, then maybe . . . I could. I mean *we* could. Max and I. Max and Minn. Our names linked together made me sigh. Made me brave enough to face any old ghost or spirit head on.

Or was it head off?

— MISSION TO ELBOW ISLAND —

There is something about the blackness of a country sky that makes me think the entire world has ducked its head underneath a blanket. The night we set out for Elbow Island it was a plush velvet sky, a shawl, maybe, studded with rhinestone stars. I thought of my mother's favourite party dress, the one she's worn at every Christmas dinner for as long as I can remember. My folks were both on my mind as I crept out the back door at Nana's. What I was doing was *wrong*. I knew this and I was doing it anyhow.

The dummy was still underneath the veranda where I'd stashed her in three green garbage bags.

"C'mon, Missy Long Johns, you've got work to do," I said to my creation. The plan was simple. I rehearsed it once again. Plant a dummy on the island with a sign that said Save the Grave! Phone the coast guard. Alert the media. Cause a stir.

It was getting out there that worried me. If someone had seen me lugging her up the road, they might have thought a murderer was on the loose, with the victim in a body bag.

This dummy was larger and more sophisticated than the one I'd made when I was eight and thrown off the balcony. She was more scarecrow than puppet. I'd stuffed her with lots of straw I'd found in the old barn, and I'd dressed her all in red, using long johns I'd bought at Harv's. That was awkward.

"What you need long johns for?" he'd asked. "It's hot as Hades these past few days."

"It's a surprise for Nana," I'd replied without blinking.

That was partly true, but I crossed my fingers anyhow. I didn't want him alerting her.

As planned, I signalled Max three times with my flashlight. He was waiting, as he'd promised, by a small dock around the corner from the government wharf. My feet echoed like a giant's as I walked towards him. He had on an orange windbreaker. Bright like neon. Some spy.

His voice was hoarse. "This way, hurry up before some dog wakes up."

We untied the rowboat and put Missy Long Johns in between us. I paddled for what seemed like forever. "It's about ten minutes until we stop," I said.

"You hope," he said. He never even offered to help row.

The distant clang of the buoys was a lonesome sound. Clang clang clang. Like a warning bell . . .

"Are you sure we should do this?" Max said.

I nodded. "Too late to turn back now!" I scanned my flashlight across the waves in front of us, a funnel of light leading only into more blackness.

The waves were choppy. The boat rocked as if it were frantic with panic. I rowed steadily until I spotted the grey hump of Elbow Island just ahead.

The rocks were giant spikes, the jagged canine teeth of some prehistoric creature. Expertly, I eased the boat into the dip we'd seen on the map. I thought Max would be impressed by that, but then we bumped up against a rock for a crash landing.

"Make sure you tie the boat tight," I said, draping Missy Long Johns around my neck and sloshing through seaweed and eelgrass until I finally reached drier land. I dumped her down at my feet and shone my flashlight around and up, trying to find a way to get over the mounds of rocks to the field beyond. Once there, I could figure out where to dump the dummy.

Yes! It was a well-worn path. Rocks almost like stair steps led out to a ledge. Easy, I thought—until I stepped on one. The rocks were slimy with algae and seaweed. Slow but steady, that was the only way to proceed. I picked up Missy Long Johns and draped her around my shoulders again. She was heavy for a scarecrow.

"Help me here, would you?" I yelled back to Max. I was high up by then and could see the field below me. "Max? Come on!"

There was no answer.

"Max?" I looked back. And saw the rowboat floating empty away from shore. "Maaaaaax!"

My own voice echoed back. Frantic, I looked ahead into the field that suddenly was like one deep black hole. Crazily, I thought maybe he had got ahead of me. But the field was empty except for clusters of scrub brush that looked like giant porcupines guarding the forest beyond. Boulders perched lopsided, ghoulish heads were sprouting from the earth, cocked to one side, taunting. Here and there, vapours spiralled up from the ground like small geysers. Swamp gas, I told myself, but if I didn't know better, I'd say they were vibrating. As if curled inside them something lived.

"Max!" I screamed. Had he fallen? "Max! Stop teasing!"

"Hey, you there!" came a reply. Not Max. A deep growl of a voice behind me.

— CHASE AND RESCUE —

"Please don't be afraid." Right.

I heard the footsteps. He was closing in.

"Turn around," he said. His voice warbled, gurgling like bubbles under water. Turn around? Not on your life.

"It's only me." Closer, closer, he was almost beside me. "John Hindley."

I ran faster than the speed of light. I shouted for Max again and again. My pleas were lost in the wind, blown out to sea, drowned by the clangs of the buoys. By this time, the sound was not just a lonesome sound but a haunting, chilling warning.

An angry wind started up. A few splats of rain hit my face.

"Max?" I whimpered. But I knew he wasn't around.

The footsteps behind me were gaining.

Once the race has started, never ever look behind you. It's a waste of valuable seconds.

The Rigbyism came out of nowhere.

"Stop!" he was shouting. "Hold on!"

I was holding on, all right. To my life. Out of his reach.

There were no clouds in the sky. No stars for guidance or light. In fact, it was like there was no sky either. I was in the midst of a mist so low to the ground, it was as if I was in the clouds. I was forced to slow down. I listened.

I'd lost him. At last. I finally threw Missy Long Johns down. And that's when the voices started. That screaming Stubby had talked about. It wasn't the wind, if that's what you're thinking. It was voices. Crying. There was no thunder. No lightning. But the rain! Like waterfalls cascading over me. I gasped for breath.

I ripped a garbage bag off Missy Long Johns and made a rain poncho for myself. The red lipstick mouth I'd been so careful with was smeared like blood all over her face. Even she looked evil.

Then, a movement in the dark. He was stalking me! I ran like I never did in my life. I was ready to break the sound barrier.

Down into the field, trying to get away from the voices and the rain and—*a ghost—a killer*.

There was nowhere to hide in the field. I had to get to the forest. I tore past the twisted-faced rocks, got snagged on spindly scrub and kept right on running. Finally I reached the woods. But his footsteps crackling through the underbrush followed.

I was in the haunted forest of my childhood night-mares. Shadows of branches like the claws of animals and the fingers of witches surrounded me. I tripped and went flying into a swampy-smelling patch of bog. I closed my eyes, expecting him to pounce. One second, two seconds, three seconds went by—like whole lifetimes.

I lifted my head, and there was a flicker of light, like a match struck and quickly blown out. He was going away. In the other direction. I lay there for five whole minutes, holding my breath as best I could. The voices were still screaming.

I stood up, staying in a crouch, and picked my way, inch by inch, along a tangled path.

Then? Well, I'd swear up and down on my own grave that I saw a woman holding a lantern. She beckoned with her arm. Steady as a beam from a lighthouse, she guided me directly to the cabin. Don't ask me how, but I knew it was the Clancy cabin. The voices started to lower as I got nearer. By the time I walked up to the front stoop, they had stopped. The stillness was worse. A deathly quiet. I stepped in as softly as I could.

"My fiancé married and had many children," she said. "He lived a happy life. I've watched now and then."

Maryanna Rayborn? It was as if she was continuing a conversation we'd started before.

"There's this this—man," I gasped. "Out there . . ."

She laughed a tinkly laugh. "There's more than one, I'm afraid. You're a sorry-looking sight." She smiled. She really was dazzling.

"And you needn't be looking so terrified. I know you've talked to spirits before. And I have to say, Miss Minn, we are all very grateful for what you are doing to save the grave. My own bones are still safely there but wouldn't have been much longer had you not taken action."

She drifted when she walked, sort of like Miss Armstrong-Blanchett, only more graceful.

"Still," she said, "before you get to saving us, there's something you need to say, is that right? There's a shadow weighing you down. I can see it plain as day all about you."

"What are you talking about?"

"Stubby told you about me. You've come here because you can whisper your darkest secret to me. I have the power to take away your shadow, your dark cloud, if you do."

"I came to save the grave."

"But you have a sad heart, am I right?"

I nodded. Gulped. Tried to swallow. There *was* a big something. I sat down. My lips moved. I began to whisper. Something like this . . .

— HARBOUR OF SECRETS —

The week before Christmas, it had snowed. And snowed and snowed and snowed. By the middle of the week, the snowbanks were so high I could prance out our back door, waddle up a snowbank and step right onto the roof of our garage.

Maybe I was a bit old to be doing what I did, but I guess that much snow would make anyone feel like a little kid again, wanting to play. Even Mr. Forest was in his yard making snowmen and forts. See, in those few minutes after I jumped off the roof and before I landed kerfluff in the white fluffy mounds below, softer than clouds, I pretended I was flying.

It's not like I was the first kid in the history of the world to imagine such a thing. Just a few summers before, Davey Stevenson had jumped off a two-storey house under construction a street away.

"What on earth could that boy have been thinking?"

my mother said, clucking and shaking her head.

"He was trying to see if he could fly," I wanted to say but didn't, knowing this was something most adults would not understand. Even one like my mother, who had a pretty lively imagination of her own. After all, it's not everyone who could come up with the name Cinnamon for a child or invent names like Mango Butter, Raspberry Riot, Grape Expectations or Paradise Pink.

"Lucky all he got was a broken arm," added Corporal Ray. "He could have gotten a concussion or worse."

Concussion. One of those words that set the bells chiming in my head. All those *s*'s shushing together in the middle like that. It was a *c* word, too, something I was collecting at the time.

"What exactly is a concussion, Dad?"

"A crack in the skull," he replied. To demonstrate, he fell to the floor, threw back his head, stuck out his tongue and started to gag. It wasn't funny, maybe, but we all laughed.

So anyhow, yes, I admit it, strange as it might sound. I spent most of the week jumping from the roof—flying! That's when I wasn't tobogganing. It was the tobogganing that caused the trouble.

The hill out back of our house was perfect—not too long a walk up and not too steep a ride down, smooth and long. You could pick up a bit of speed, too, if you happened to be brave enough to go over the ramp we made.

For Christmas I'd gotten a new toboggan. It was a two-seater wooden one from Canadian Tire—the exact one I asked for. And could it race down that hill!

Most days we took turns, lining up patiently until it was our time to slide down. Up and down all day on that hill we zoomed and slid, until finally the sun started to dip behind the houses on the next street and blue shadows filled the yard. Only then did we realize it was close to supper and we'd all turned into human icicles and thoughts of steaming mugs of hot chocolate made us head for the warmth of our houses.

Our fun came to an end when Davey Stevenson came back from Florida with his sunburned face orange as a pumpkin. His sled was black plastic with silver chrome. He hogged the whole hill, taking more turns than anybody, pushing some of the smaller kids out of the way, washing some of the girls' faces with snow.

"I'll bet my sled goes faster than that old-fashioned wooden piece of junk," he said to me.

"Bet it doesn't," I snapped back.

"Bet you're too chicken too race."

"Bet I'm not!"

The Robichaud twins, Rita and Renette, said on yer mark get set go! and we flew down the hill. I won!

I should have let it go at that—I see this now, of course. At the time, though, Davey was bugging me too much. Besides, we had a long history, years of getting underneath each other's skin.

"Girls are better than boys!" I shouted out in a singsongy voice, rubbing it in.

Everyone laughed. His sunburn reddened. Sunburn Blush! I'd have to tell my mother about this one for sure.

"Cinnamon Hog-kiss!" said Davey and snorted like a pig. He kissed the air with loud smacking noises.

He yanked the toboggan rope out of my mittened hands and ran up to the top of the hill. I tried to follow. You're not likely to break any records for speed when you try running uphill weighted down by all your winter gear. I couldn't catch up in time, I knew this. My mind worked fast enough, though, and I saw a way to stop him.

Everyone said what happened next was like watching a movie in slow motion.

Davey took a running start and hit the toboggan with his stomach and blasted off. He careened down the hill. When he got to the middle and the little jump that made you really fly into the air, I jumped on. I started thwacking him on the back.

Instead of veering to the left to go down by the side of our house and out onto the sidewalk, the toboggan boomeranged to the right. I rolled off. Davey kept on going. And smashed right through our basement window. And landed in the furnace. Well, almost. When we

reached him, there was glass everywhere and red pinpricks on the snow that led to a big splotch of blood. I
remember thinking that blood on snow was the reddest
red I had ever seen. Blood on Snow. My mother would
never use that! Before I knew it, my mother was there,
shoving her way through the circle of kids.

"Rita, Renette!" she screamed. "Get your mother to
call the ambulance!"

We all watched as my mother grunted and groaned
and pulled off the whole window frame. Then, with all
her might, she pulled Davey, toboggan and all, back
through the opening. His skull must be cracked this
time for sure, I thought. There was blood coming from
his nose, too.

Davey was howling, and my mother sat right down
in the snow, cradling his head in her lap. She only had
on a pair of sweats and a skimpy sweater that didn't
stretch all the way over her belly. On her feet were the
fluffy pink bunny slippers I'd given her for Christmas.
Her ankles had to be freezing, I was thinking. And
what about the baby inside her? Could the baby feel the
cold too?

But my mother didn't seem to notice. She just kept
rocking Davey as if he was a baby, back and forth, until
the ambulance arrived.

At supper, we found out that Davey had a concussion
all right, and "a broken nose to boot," said Corporal Ray.

"He's going to be fine, just fine." He even tried to make a joke about it.

If you take Cinnamon's flying toboggan
You'll break your nose and crack your noggin.

"Ray, it's no laughing matter," said my mother. She was lying on the couch with her feet up on a cushion. "There will be no more tobogganing out back. We know now it's just too dangerous."

So that would have been enough bad news for the week and I felt guilty as anything over what happened to Davey's head. But then . . .

"Yes?" said Miss Rayborn. "What else?"

"I can't."

"You must continue."

"It's too horrible."

"Whisper softer if you have to."

So I did. I understood then why she called herself the Woman of Whispers. See, the worst things we have done in our lives, the worst thoughts, can't really come out in a normal voice. Stubby was right. Instead, it's more like breathing the thoughts out, like small gusts of wind, a poisonous breeze. So I whispered even softer.

In the middle of the night, the same night as Davey's accident, I woke up to hear my mother crying out. The sound! It was a cross between the whimpering of a dog and the piercing cry of a bird.

My father rushed into my bedroom. "Wake up!" he shouted. "Hurry up, Minn!" He was almost shaking me. "I have to take your mother to the hospital—now! Get your coat."

He dialled Mrs. Robichaud as I ran for my coat. It was like a dream and I kept thinking I would wake up. I peeked in the bedroom on my way downstairs. I saw blood—a splash of pink on their white sheets.

When Mrs. Robichaud took me to her house, she sat me down in her kitchen and made me cinnamon toast.

"Not to worree it will be all right, everyting will be okay." She was fingering the beads of her rosary as she told me this.

Later, she tucked me into bed with the twins. Even in their sleep, they were identical, breathing in time with each other. I tried to match my breathing to theirs and pretended I was a triplet.

The next day my father told me that the baby—my sister—was dead.

The Woman of Whispers was hugging herself, her arms folded tight across her chest.

"I killed my sister," I whispered. "I'm the reason she died. It was me who took Davey up on his bet. It was me who made him so mad he took my toboggan. It was me who jumped on the toboggan and made him crash through the window. If I had just shut up. If it wasn't for me, my mother would never have lifted off that window

frame and lugged him like that. I killed Pippa and my
mother will never be the same again. Ever."

All those tears I couldn't let out that night with Harv
came gushing out then. My sad throat feeling flooded
my whole body, my chest, my belly, behind my eyes.

Miss Rayborn said nothing. When my loud messy
blubbering slowed down to little hiccupy sobs, she
stood up.

She waved her arms in a circle and the cabin door
blew open with a bang. It was a lot like Stubby told me.
A cloud drifted in through the door. The Woman of
Whispers circled my head with her arms and whispered
into the cloud. Then she blew softly, as if fanning a fire.
The cloud changed colour, from layers of wispy white
fog into a cloud of soot. A rain cloud. It drifted out and
the door slammed shut.

I can't say I felt any better.

"Next time it rains, you will," she said. I guess she
could read thoughts, too.

"Minn," she continued in a whisper, "you must tell
your mother."

"Never!"

"Trust me."

Before I could argue, there were heavy, thudding footsteps on the porch. I froze.

"There you are!" That voice!

I screamed and turned to Miss Rayborn.

She was gone.

He wobbled in the door, holding an axe. "Minn," he said.

"Please, I have my whole life ahead of me!"

"My name's John Hindley," he said.

"So you said."

"Pleased to make your acquaintance," he said and shook my hand. His touch was like a feather tickle. His eyes were the eyes I had in my photo. Only older and glazed.

I looked at the axe.

"It's just for the woodpile, miss." He leaned it against the wall.

And then? John Hindley talked. And talked. He told me his story.

When he was through I didn't know what to say. His story was more tragic than the few dry lines in the newspaper accounts. He wouldn't tell me much at all about his new life after he left for New York.

"Maybe some other time. You've heard enough for one night. But I must tell you this, Miss Minn. You have given me such a gift in saving the grave."

"But I haven't done it yet!"

"You have. But more than that, thanks to you, my brother and I have found our way back to each other. It takes the living to reunite the dead sometimes." He pointed towards the door.

Standing in the door frame was a shadow. I peered into the darkness. The shadow floated closer.

"Cucurbita MAXima! Where have you been?" I shouted. "And ... And ..."

I looked back at John. "What did you say?"

"Minn." Max stepped towards me. He held me close. He sighed. "My name isn't Max. It's Thomas. Thomas Hindley."

I stuttered and blubbered. I looked back and forth between the two. I tried to swallow. The resemblance between them was unmistakable. Striking! Those eyes.

I pounded Max's chest. "Stop this now! It's not a joke any more! You can't be. You're real. *See?*" I hit him again. He winced.

"I'm real to you," he said. "And that's what counts." I kicked him again—in the shin—and ran for the door.

The floor crumbled beneath my feet. All I remember was a sinking feeling, a horrible weightlessness as I fell through space. Down. Deep down. The smell of wet earth. Rotting seaweed. Sinking, falling, flying, dying? Mum, Dad, Nana, Harv, Carolina, Davey, Coach Rigby, John Hindley. Jumping down from the mizzen rigging into the frigid waves. Max. Thomas? Then no thoughts. No pictures. Black nothingness. Nightmare Black.

— NEW CONFESSIONS —

Blue. Baby blue. Periwinkle blue. The blankets cover-ing me and the walls around me were that kind of blue. At the foot of my bed was a semicircle of dark blue shapes that wobbled. Mum, Dad, Nana, Harv— I recognized them, but it was like I was looking through the windshield of a car going through a car wash, the glass dripping with water thick as petro-leum jelly.

"Mum?" Pushing the word out took effort, as if it was sticking to my parched lips.

"My baby, my baby." She was by side, smelling like lavender soap, kissing my cheeks, her cheek like velvet against mine.

Nana grabbed one hand and Harv stood beside her. Corporal Ray came to the other side of the bed and ran his fingers over my eyelids.

"Oh, Minn," my mother said.

That's the only memory I have until a nurse woke me up saying, "Drink this."

She put a glass to my lips. I sipped through a bendy straw. It hurt to swallow. I couldn't move one arm. My head felt like hundreds of fairies with spurs on their heels danced on the top of my skull.

"Your parents are out in the hall. Want me to send them in?"

"Just my mother."

If I was about to die, I needed to tell her.

"How's your arm?" she asked first thing.

"Plaster White," I whispered.

"Goofball," she said.

"What happened, Mum? How did I get here?"

"Harv and another man—a camper out on Elbow Island—rescued you. You've been unconscious for a bit."

"Am I going to die?"

"Not unless your grandmother kills you."

"Am I ever going to run again?"

"Cut the melodrama, Minn. There's not a thing wrong with your legs. Thank God, it's just your arm and a concussion."

That shushy word.

So I wasn't going to die. Maybe I didn't have to tell her anything.

"I'm really not going to die?"

"Not a chance. But oh, the risk you took!"

"Guess you're pretty mad, hey?"

"Molten Lava Red Mad. Also relieved, exasperated, guilty."

"Guilty?"

"We never should have sent you away for the summer."

"It wasn't so bad, leastways now that it's almost over." I winced as I tried to laugh. "Mum, I have . . . I have to tell you something."

"I'm listening," she said.

It hit me. She *was*. Listening like she used to. Her eyes looking into mine. So I began.

It took a long time, because the words were still sticking to the roof of my mouth. I thought of Stubby searching for words. I felt a bit like that.

"So. Now you know. I'm sorry. The baby." For a while the only sound was my own breathing.

Then she grabbed my good hand and squeezed so tight I figured I'd need another cast when she was through.

"Oh, Minn. All this time that's what you've thought? Look—we didn't tell you what really happened because . . . well, I guess we wanted to protect you. We thought it was too terrible to tell you. So we said it was just a miscarriage . . . which in a way it was."

"What are you saying?"

"Minn, the baby had already died, at least ten days before then. It wasn't because of Davey's accident. If anything, it might have gone on longer and I could have been in real danger."

"You mean . . ." I shuddered. "The baby was dead, inside you?"

"Yes. And . . . I think I knew, too. I felt something was wrong. She'd stopped kicking."

No wonder she had been lost for so long in that silence.

"Where is she, Mum. The baby? What do you do with a baby that died just before it was born? You never told me that either!" I was fuming.

"We had her cremated. She's, um . . . in a vase in the china cabinet." I suddenly understood the dusting obsession she had. Why she was so fanatic about that old china cabinet. It was the only thing she did all winter.

"You should have told me the whole truth, nothing but the truth cross my h-heart, h-hope to d-die s-stick a needle—I *was* old enough!" I screamed.

The nurse rushed in. She rubbed my forehead until I fell asleep again. "Shh, honey, calm down" was the last thing I heard my mother say.

I had a new Pippa dream. This time, I was flying through the night sky on my toboggan. My sister angel was very alive and beside me.

— FAME AND SHAME —

"Smile!"

"Could you repeat that again, looking into this camera?"

The media had descended upon Boulder Basin. They came right into my room to snap photos of me with my cast and turban of bandages. I did an interview for TV for *Live at Five* and the CBC. Imagine, me on CBC radio! The woman who interviewed me had wild red hair. First she scolded me for doing what I did and putting my life at risk. "I'm a mother and you'd be grounded for life if you were mine," she said, but with a huge grin.

All the media attention made me think of how John Hindley must have felt in New York City. I'd read in my research that the New York media called him Miracle Boy and hounded him. Thoughts of that night and what he'd told me kept drifting in and out of my dreams.

"Enough," my father finally said. "You've had your fifteen minutes of fame."

Nana gushed about what was happening down at Riley Tucker's office.

"Apparently," she said, "somebody dumped bones at his office doorstep! Imagine!"

I gawked at her. Or was it Max?

Everybody thought I'd taken the boat out myself.

"I didn't," I told them.

"Who was with you?" Corporal Ray was furious.

"I never knew his real name," I told them. "He's left town. Just some guy." I shrugged.

Harv patted my hand. "Don't be heartbroken over a lad that won't give you his name and leaves town first sign of trouble. Besides, he's not the only fish in the sea." I winced. Bad choice of words.

And I didn't escape Nana's tongue-lashing when she figured I was recovered enough to hear.

"Stupid! That's what it was! A stupid, stupid stunt! Foolhardy! A rapscallion! That's what you are. A rapscallion! Good word for you! You might think I'm some old obstreperous curmudgeon, but that is nothing compared to you!"

"My head hurts, Nana!" I protested, hoping that would shut her up.

"Good, I hope it aches for a good while yet! Every time it does, may you reflect on what you've done! If you weren't lying there I'd take a hickory switch to your behind, that's what I'd be doing if you were my child! Harv risked his life for you. Imagine!"

Harv had been the brave one to figure out where I'd headed and went out in the middle of the night to Elbow Island. My hero. With the way the wind had kicked up, the coast guard had advised against it. And he got to me anyhow. And that other man—this camper who *prefers to remain anonymous*, the papers said—had already found me after I fell through the rotting floorboards of the Clancy cabin.

"He and Harv got you to the hospital in record time." Nana repeated her version of events every time she came to visit. There I was, alone in the room with the Vinegar Witch, at her mercy. Oh yeah, the witch wasn't long resurfacing! The whole room turned sour with every breath she took. Vapours of oatmeal and Lux soap mixed up together. Nana Vinegar was on a roll.

I was relieved when visiting hours were over. But that didn't put a stop to visitations.

Thomas—Max—crept sideways into my room. He looked at me as though I'd spring from my bed and attack him at any moment. I would have if I could have!

"How are you?"

"Tickety-boo. What's it look like?"

"I am sorry, Minn, I am. I never meant . . ."

I turned my face to the wall.

"You had to do it alone but you couldn't be completely alone . . . so I was there for moral support . . ."

He showed me a headline in a provincial newspaper:

13-YEAR-OLD GIRL A GRAVESAVER!

"That's you—a gravesaver!" There was my face below a map of Elbow Island and a picture of the SS *Atlantic*. I began to read.

> Due to the persistence and daring of a 13-year-old from Fairvale, the gravesite of the SS Atlantic will be restored. Intending to plant a decoy on Elbow Island to draw attention to the eroding grave, Cinnamon Elizabeth Hotchkiss was stranded for a few harrowing hours—

I tossed it aside.

"Whatever," I said. And I'm *almost* thirteen! And you . . . used me! You needed *me* to get to John, right?"

"Is that so bad? I've missed him for the longest time. He wouldn't come any closer than Elbow Island because he blamed himself for . . . well, for living. We wasted a lot of time. I brought you something."

"Just go, okay?"

But he didn't. "Take this first." He opened his hand. In his palm was a rock. "It's yours," he said. "It belongs to you, I think."

A heart-shaped rock. A white one.

"I found it yesterday," he said. "It's still a little crooked."

"It's perfect," I managed to croak out as he put it into my hand. But his hand did not touch mine. Still, he got close enough so I could smell that fresh-air smell about him.

"Yes, well." He cleared his throat. "If I were a young lad now, I want you to know . . ."

Then he leaned down and, yes, kissed me. *On the lips.*

"Gotta go. But this isn't farewell. Not yet."

He kissed me again.

He tasted like oranges.

❧ No Happy Ever After ❧

The longer I lived, the more I wanted my family back. The more I missed having an older brother. I guess the truth is I drank and I fought.

I once dreamed of being an engineer and designing a bridge, something that carried people safely across the water. Instead, I quit school and went to work on the Brooklyn Bridge. Wasn't afraid one bit of falling. Those suspension cables were just like the rigging. I was still scared of water, though. So I held on tight and did a fine job.

I never fell in love or married or had children.

At times I'd think of finding my way back to Nova Scotia and living a simple life.

Sometimes I scribbled poems. The night I died, I wrote this one.

Where is the boy from Ashton gone, the laughing boy with

his heart still young?
Where is the boy who loved to live? Well he died the night
  his brother drowned.
Where is the hope that sorrow ends? When did pain
  become my friend?
Where has the sun decided to hide? Deep down in the sea
  where my brother died.
And the tide comes in and the tide goes out
And I get up every morn
And my brother died when just a lad
And I wish I'd never been born.
And I wish I'd never been born.

So you see, I'm no shining example of how you overcome
disaster. Is that what you thought? I survived the best I
could for as long as I could.

I watch now from this place and I like to think I've
learned a lot. I've seen how some folks go through things,
and they not only survive, they go forward and thrive.

I am no hero. Heroes are people who never give up hope.
No matter what. Giving up is never an answer. I didn't that
night on the mizzen. But I did eventually, and drowned in
my own sorrow.

I was twenty-two years old the day they opened the
Brooklyn Bridge. I celebrated a bit too much. For the
record—so you'll know—I stumbled. I didn't jump.

But when I heard the train, I didn't move, either. The

railroad ties underneath me looked like a ladder. I hung on like it was the mizzen.

It was instant.

Decapitation.

— UNEXPECTED KINDNESSES —

Next morning, after the bedpans and sponge bath, I was told I had more visitors. The chauffeur ambled into my room. He twisted the brim of his hat nervously in his hands. His hair was so silver I wanted to touch it to make sure it was real. He wasn't wearing sunglasses.

I have a thing for eyes, I guess. His were kind and sea glass green. He wasn't as old as I thought. His smile was charming. To think I thought he was a drug smuggler. You have to get close to people to know them. There is so much you can't tell from a distance.

"Minn, I'm Paul Dubbins."

The shock must have registered on my face. Paul Dubbins was a famous artist.

"We met briefly. I rent the Fullerton place. I'm an artist."

"You are?" I said. "I mean, I know."

"Let me guess." He smiled. "You were thinking I was Hardly Whynot's driver, right?"

I nodded. "You said you wanted my picture for an album."

He laughed and slapped his thigh. "A *photo* album! I sometimes paint from photos. And I'd still like yours."

"Bad hair day," I said.

"So it *was* you!" he exclaimed.

"Me?"

"The informer. The other day these four women came to my house asking for my boss's autograph. They were most disappointed to discover I was not the chauffeur for the famous singer of the Ladybugs. They told me some young girl had told them I was his driver."

I know I turned red as my hot water bottle. "Well, there's always been this rumour, and I was hoping to get his autograph. For my mother."

"Gave me a good enough laugh. How about you take my autograph on this?"

He handed me a cheque. There were a lot of zeros. It was made out to The SS *Atlantic* Heritage Project.

"Oh. My," I managed to mumble. "Thank you," I said. And then into the room burst the Cackleberry Women with huge bouquets of flowers.

"Ladies, good day," Paul Dubbins said and winked at me as he was leaving.

"Sooo cute," one whispered to the other. "Rich and famous. Your Nana was right," sighed another.

The Cackleberry Women turned out to be nice as

anything. They fussed. One kissed me. They said they'd donate some money too. Then they were gone. Their perfume lingered.

Nana bristled back into the room and immediately sneezed. "Uppity Canadians! Hospitals are supposed to be scent-free zones!" No doubt she was going to continue her lecture on my harbour of stupidity.

I handed her the cheque signed by Mr. Dubbins.

She looked at it. Her eyes were wide as pie plates.

"But," I said, taking the cheque away, "you might not want it—seeing as he's a CFA."

Then she leaned over me, sour old witch, so close I could have bitten off those three chin hairs.

"I have never, ever known a child to harbour such hope and determination in her heart," she said.

Then she kissed my cheek. And smiled. She didn't smell sour at all.

— HOME AGAIN, JIGGETY JIG! —

"You idiot! You total idiot!" Carolina had a new haircut and was brown as a berry. "I could have lost my best friend ever in the world!" She burst into tears.

"Now who's being melodramatic?" But I hugged her tight and started blatting too. My father mumbled something about hormones and left the room with my mother.

Getting home meant telling everything to her. Well, almost everything.

"Whatever happened to that cutie you met?"

"Oh yeah. He was a real dream," I said.

"What happened?" she squealed. "Did you kiss? Mouth open?"

"Ew. Carolina! No! We did *not* kiss. Not like that."

"Oh you! Only Minn! You're still such a tomboy!"

No, I wanted to say, I'm *Tom's girl*.

"Once you've had a real kiss, you'll know! I do, I do!" And she started to tell me the details. Like something

278

out of one of her bodice-ripper romances. She calls me a snob when I tell her those books are so much garboon. She says she's sure I'll grow into them!

Even to Carolina, I couldn't tell the deepest secret of my heart.

At least she was interested in what happened. She pored over the old articles about the shipwreck from the *Boulder Basin Bulletin*. Nana had given me photocopies the day I left.

It was good to get back home and see her and the neighbourhood and all things familiar. Familiar but changed.

The baby's room was gone, for one thing. It was a cedar-lined storage closet instead. But my room was different as well. They'd placed a cradle in a corner of my room. It was filled with my old stuffed animals and a few dolls. "If you want it?" my mother said.

"Where did you guys find this, anyway?" I asked her.

"A friend of your grandmother's attic. It's really old."

When she was gone, I crawled underneath it. Sure enough. Scratched out and faded were the initials P. H.

Patrick Hindley? I wanted to scream and cry and laugh. Everything and nothing made sense.

Mr. Forest, who was still taking it easy because of his angina, came to visit me with books galore. One was a science book on clouds. I searched that book page by page. Nowhere did the book suggest that clouds were spirits.

So I had no scientific proof for anything—no rational explanation. So then I read all the Harry Potters. They made more sense. We rented the DVD of *Titanic*.

Coach Rigby brought me chocolates. And some more Rigbyisms to try to cheer me up because I wasn't allowed to run. I pleaded and screamed with my parents. I cursed many benedictuses. All to no good. I begged Coach Rigby. He handed me another Rigbyism.

There is no such thing as failure as long as you
answer this question: Because of what you've learned,
what next?

"Where do you get these from, fortune cookies?" I snarled. He looked hurt. "Sorry," I said. I still had harbours of mean thoughts and actions.

He shook his head and left. I felt like a snivelling brat. I was. I looked at his Rigbyism again. What comes next? As a runner, I was washed up. I am a failure, I decided.

Then one day, when I was feeling real sorry for myself, I looked up *minikin*. It was a real word. It made me feel a whole lot better.

School started, and life almost seemed normal. But how, really, would it ever be normal?

— PROPER BURIALS —

We picked out a tombstone for Pippa. It was a statue of a little girl I found at a flea market.

"It's a lawn ornament, honey," said Corporal Ray. Delicate as could be.

"No, Ray, it's perfect," said my mother. She hugged me.

So we brought it home and made a new flower bed in the backyard. We dug deep, with our hands, and placed the vase of ashes ever so gently down into the earth.

We cried a little.

Corporal Ray carved a wooden plaque for her. "Pippa" is all it says.

Maybe a lot of people would think it morbid to bury the ashes of an unborn child in your own backyard. I personally think Pippa loves it there, especially when the sunflowers bloom among the pink and purple cosmos.

Besides, in Boulder Basin there was a woman who buried her miniature schnauzer in her front yard. She put a white wrought-iron fence all around it. The tomb-stone read: "Fergus—loyal dog and friend."

There are no limits to how important it is to mark the passing of the dead from one world to the next, no matter where you might believe they end up. Or even if you believe.

We have a bench by Pippa's burial spot, too. We can visit her whenever we want. I still remember John telling me that sometimes it takes the living to reunite the dead.

Sometimes, it takes the dead to reunite the living, too.

— ABSENCE MAKES THE HEART —

A lot more than the Isthmus of Chignecto—say that fast three times—separates the province of Nova Scotia from the province of New Brunswick. Fairvale was home sweet home but I missed the sound of gulls, the salty air, the lap of waves.

My mother kept telling me I had to find the time to write Nana a nice little thank you note. Thank her for what exactly?

Then one Saturday afternoon, Mum and Corporal Ray were cutting up cucumbers and making mustard pickles. The kitchen was filled with a vinegar smell so strong it made my eyes water. Before I knew what I was doing, I'd picked up my pen.

DEAR NANA,
Well, it's been a month since I've been home and I thought I should catch you up with the news. I know how

283

you hate to talk on the phone and so I am writing. Hope you can read this letter okay. My hand is still wobbly!

I am bursting to know what is happening with the restoration plan. How is Harv doing? Have you had many clients?

The doctor and Corporal Ray and Mum, even Coach Rigby, would not let me compete in the provincials. I felt just fine! Raring to go, in fact. So I went to the track and watched from the sidelines. The winner of the 100 metres had a slower time than my last best! That first-place ribbon should have been mine! Oh well. Like Coach Rigby said, there's a reason for everything and there's always next year. Still, all that work and all that training.

Mum and Dad are fine. Finer than fine, actually. Things seem normal around here again. No more Kraft Dinner! Mum has gone back to work at the paint store. This fall, she's really on an orange craze. How many ways could you describe orange, you must be thinking. Least I know I did. Well, how about Orange Sparkle, Organic Orange, Orange Tequila! That's Mexican orange, she told me. Then there's Sunburst Orange, Ember Orange and Mandarin Orange. I knew she was really feeling better when she came up with Ya-Ya-Yam! Between you and me, I can't tell much difference between any of them, but with all her mixing and matching, I guess there must be something the trained eye can pick up.

Anyhow, she's humming happy Ladybugs songs again. Between her shrieks and Corporal Ray's yodels, I feel like I'm living in an audition hall. I'd say she's put last winter far from her mind. Anyhow, hope all is well and write when you can.

Yours truly,
Minn

DEAR MINN,
Orange! I'd feel like I was living inside a piece of Canadian cheddar if I painted a room orange.

I am sorry to hear about your track meet. No one knows more than I do how hard you worked, although half the time I figured you were just running away from me. Still, with a stunt like you pulled you needed some sort of consequence to teach you not to go doing anything so foolish ever again in your life!

Some days I still get in a wicked rage thinking about what you did! You are one stubborn young lady! Then again, I suppose it runs in the family. (Harv told me I had to write that in.)

The exciting news is how fast things are coming together. Thanks to that generous contribution Mr. Dubbins made, I guess other folks were almost ashamed and started putting in their two cents' worth. Even though you scared the Kapoopsie out of all of us, your plan worked, Minn. We are aiming for an official opening next July. Imagine! We are even going to invite the premier.

Well, I might as well not be coy about my own big news. Hang on to your hat—I said yes to Harv's most recent proposal of marriage! You should have seen his face. He went white as a ghost. I had a great chuckle. Then I was worried. Thinking maybe I'd turned him down so long he never meant what he was asking, you know what I mean? See, what I never wanted to tell him was that the main reason I always said no was I did not want to be married to that store. It ran his whole life! I'm not a real sociable kind of person and the thought that I might have to go help out and pump gas and smile at those come from aways—not on your life! Well, he's been thinking about selling that store and now there's someone who's made him a pretty good offer. I figured it would be nice to spend our life more together than apart. The truth is, Minn, this summer I thought I was going to lose the two people I loved most in the world in one night. Besides your father, I mean. So better make hay while the sun shines. We're going to Nunavut for our honeymoon. I've always wanted to see the North and the aurora borealis.

We thought we'd get hitched as they say around here about the same time as the official opening of the SS *Atlantic* Heritage Site. You folks will be here, and so will Harv's children. So it will be a good party, eh? I'm going to start cooking soon! I haven't told your parents yet. I have a request. Could you read this letter out loud to them for me. Thank you.

Your grandmother, the bride to be

P.S. Enclosed is a package that came addressed to you from England. Yes, I wanted to snoop, but I didn't. Cross my heart.

DEAR NANA,
YOU AND HARV! Congratulations!!! YEAH!!! And more good news! You will never guess! Mr. Dubbins is going to do a special portrait in time for the ceremony!

But even more exciting than that! Mr. Dubbins somehow got Hardly Whynot's autograph for Mum! It is a picture of him when he was younger and that is a good thing. That is how Mum likes him best. In the lower left-hand corner it says: To Dory, with love and best wishes, Hardly Whynot. Can you believe that? Turns out Mr. Dubbins said he had a friend of a friend of a friend of a friend of a friend and so on who had the means to get it!

Mum screamed like she was on *MuchMusic* and pulled at her hair! Weird! That night Dad brought home an old photo of himself all blown up. On it he had written: To Dory, with love and best wishes, your true love, Ray! He put it on the dresser beside old Hardly. They laughed like kids. Then they played "I'm in Love with You You

You" (the Hardly version) and danced. It was really sucky.
Sorry I know you don't like that word. It was though. Big
time. But it made my heart burst all the same.

Here comes the bride, dum dum dee dum.

Your granddaughter,
Minn

❧

Truth be told, Nana and me got along a lot better apart
than we did when we were together. I'm pretty sure she had
something to do with me being asked to be a speaker at the
official opening of the SS *Atlantic* Heritage Site. I almost
said no because I had never spoken in public before. But
then my father said, Think before you decide, and my
mother said she'd help me practice and then Nana sent this:

❧

DEAR MINN,
Thought you should see the enclosed letter, which
turned up in my friend Mabel's attic. She was related to
the Clancys who lived in the cabin out on Elbow Island.
The one you almost got yourself killed in. Looks like a
letter from the one boy who survived the disaster. Did
you get around to reading the article on him I had? It
was in a Moirs Pot of Gold box. There is even a picture.

We are getting lots of other artifacts for the interpreta-
tion centre. A beautiful knife showed up the other day,
rusted of course, but the case is gorgeous.

September 27, 1873

Dear Mrs. Clancy:
You asked me to write and let you know how things
were here in New York City. As you kindly cautioned
me, my arrival here was both bitter and sweet. To see
my sisters again was a joy. It was a tearful reunion.
Then there was something to contend with I had not
anticipated. We were intruded upon, rudely at times,
by the press. At Grand Central Depot, they were
waiting. My sister called them vultures. To make a
curiosity out of me and not give our family adequate
time for our grief was, she said, like picking at the
bones of the dead. They took a photograph of me. I
am so shocked looking in that picture I shall not send
it to you. That nice man in Halifax has a better one.
Perhaps he might send one to me?
    The mayor of New York City extended an official
welcome to me. I was given a tour along the Hudson
River and of City Hall and then the Stock Exchange.
I am sorry to say that when I arrived there, something happened. I had a spell. Being there amidst all
that confusion, I was swept back to the night on ship.
I ran around confused until I collapsed.

The other event is almost funny to me now. Mr P.
T. Barnum wanted me to join his travelling show! He
was ready to have me travel from town to town on a
train and jump into a pool of water. He offered
money. I said no but I was quite pleased to meet him,
as my friend Ryan would have wanted that!

I quite like my teacher. His name is Mr. O'Riley
and his Irish accent puts me in mind of my father.
He makes learning fun, too, although he is particular
about us doing our very best. Lately, he has been
giving me extra books he thinks I can learn from, as
I am mightily bored with what we do in school most
oft. These books are written by a Mr. Peter Parley
and he makes geography an exciting tale rather than
facts one has to learn. I especially like the verses Mr.
Parley has penned at the beginning of each lesson.

And there is something to rejoice about. Bridgit's
baby was born, and a big strapping lad he'll be. He
has those bean black eyes of my father and the goodly
natured grin of my brother's, I swear. They have bap-
tized him Patrick Thomas Hindley.

Each day on my return from school, I play with
him while Bridgit fixes supper. I rock him for Ma.
I feel her presence with me often then. Then I think
of you—I hope your baby is snug in my father's
cradle. I'm flattered you called him John. As I was
flattered and honoured at your offer of adoption.

But I knew my place was here with my family.

Sometimes, I recite poems to Bridgit's baby I remember and new ones I am learning. This calms my own nerves as well before I sleep. Sometimes, I am still prone to spells of passing out, and the nightmares continue, but less so.

To arrive in the city of my dreams without my folks and brother is not the way it should be. But school has started and so, it seems, has my new life. There is much to learn and yes, still, so much to forget.

Sometimes, I wake up in the darkest part of the night and shadows seem to swallow me like the waves of that ocean. I swear I can hear the moaning of the ship's rafters beneath me, the roar of that murderous sea, and the wailing of the dying. I cry then—a sea of tears upon my pillow. Quiet as I can for fear of waking up the baby and my family, the one I now have left.

I miss them all, of course. My mother, Thomas, even Ryan, a friend of such short duration. He pops in and out of my reveries from time to time doing his jig and bowing and tipping his hat. This memory makes me laugh and those are in short enough supply. Yet I have learned something about memory. We can select what comes forth. We can. I have learned also that in this life, one does not want to know what the future holds. For if we could, we might not have courage to go another day. And we must.

*It is my father whose face returns to me most
often—his face that night he burst in through the
door holding those tickets in his fist like bits of gold. I
see the light shine in his eyes and feel the warmth of
his arms as I run and jump up and he hugs me in,
scratching my face with the stubble of whiskers on his
chin. I smell the tobacco and ale and the wind in
March. The joy. I can feel it. And every time I do,
I am no longer afraid. Or alone.*

*Forgive my indulgence in writing details that might
bore you. I will always feel close to you, as without
your care I might have perished. Thanks for remembering me and please remember me to your family and
Boulder Basin folks. Also, I wish to thank you for
paying visits to the cemetery and placing flowers there
on my behalf. Please pass on my fondest regards to
Mr. Rev. William Ancient. I'm not sure I adequately
thanked him for saving my life. He is a true hero.*

John Hindley

I began writing a poem about Reverend Ancient for the
creative writing class Miss Armstrong-Blanchett started
in the winter. It was coming out like a love poem so I
gave up. I thought I'd go to you-know-where writing like
you-know-what to a man like that. He was a hero but he
was also a minister. And old. Ancient, like his name.

Nana phoned and asked me to be her maid of honour and I said yes I'd be honoured. Then I discussed with my mother if there was any way I could bring up the subject of electrolysis delicately and if Honeymoon Passion would be a good shade of lipstick with the magenta pantsuit Nana said she'd be wearing. I wrote and complained about having to shave my legs and armpits and about a friend of my mother's who had to wax her mustache. If she didn't take that hint, she never would.

So everything was just tickety-boo and humming along and I was feeling ready for spring practice and every day was a Zippity Do Da day just the way Corporal Ray sang it.

After everything I'd gone through, I really should have known better.

—LIVING-ROOM NEWS—

"We want to talk to you in the living room, Minn."

Just the tone of Corporal Ray's voice warned me something was up. I was hot and sweaty after track practice. It was too humid for May.

"Can I shower, first?"

"Better not."

My mother was in there already, on the sofa, blowing her nose.

Corporal Ray cleared his throat. He pulled his chair up to where I was sitting, his kneecap touching mine.

"Minn, give me your hands."

For a split second there I imagined they were going to tell me they had reconsidered and were going to adopt after all and I would have a baby brother or sister one day. My O.I. was wrong.

When I was seven, I saw a border collie pup get hit by a half-ton truck. He spun around like the dial on

Wheel of Fortune before skidding to a stop. His eyes were open and he was motionless. Except when I touched him, I felt a twitch. He was still breathing. Corporal Ray picked him up and carried him to our car, and I held him in my lap all the way to the vet's. And wonder of wonders, he recovered. The owners reclaimed him and it was a story with a happy ending.

But that day in the living room, Corporal Ray had not one ray of hope to give me: "Harv Jollymore passed away in his sleep."

I learned that day that unexpected news could hit you with the force of a half-ton truck. A monster truck. The shock of sorrowful news can be violent and just has its way with you until it is done.

We went to Boulder Basin for the funeral service at St. John the Baptist Anglican Church.

"He was a man well loved and it was a life well lived," they said. This was true. But those words didn't take away the plain truth and that hole in your belly feeling.

Entering Nana's kitchen when we first got there was one of the hardest things I ever had to do in my life. It was quiet. No radio blaring. The kitchen smelled like boiled tea.

There were enough casseroles on the countertops to feed a small village. Nana was staring out the window. She looked old and tired and little. When she stood up and came towards me, I realized I was taller than her. I hugged her so tight I hoped my heart could touch hers for a second or two and she would know how sorry I was for her loss. And mine. I couldn't seem to find my voice.

And anyhow, sometimes, words are totally useless.

—FINAL PREPARATIONS—

Nana seemed in good spirits this morning. We arrived at her place late last night but I was so nerved up about the ceremony I had a hard time sleeping. She brought me in some tea and talked a bit about her upcoming trip to Nunavut. She was taking Mabel-up-the-road with her.

We had porridge for breakfast, fed the gulls toast crumbs and then all of us started getting ready all at once. Nana barged into my bedroom to put her ironing board away and caught me rehearsing my speech in the mirror.

"Relax, Minn, you'll do fine."

"But even the premier—" I began.

"He's only a person," she interrupted. "And a misguided one at that."

"What do you mean by that?"

"It means she didn't vote for him." Corporal Ray clomped in then, dressed in his red serge. He looked spiffy.

"I bet Betty Meisner R.N. will think you're still a dream boat," I said.

"Spit," he replied and pointed to the toe of his boot. I hawked a good one.

"Well that's certainly attractive," said Nana as he started polishing.

Mum breezed into the room in pistachio green. "Does anyone have to go before we go?"

"No," said three of us in unison.

"I wonder if other families have a pee-checker before they leave for special occasions?" I mumbled. Perhaps they would sense my increasing irritation at their intrusion.

"It could be just a Maritime thing," said Nana.

"No, I'm pretty sure all Canadians do it"

"It could even be a North American thing."

"Americans would never do that."

"Sure they would—Oh-h say have you pe-"

"Ray, that's awful."

"Funny though."

"As for the British?"

"Have we had our little piddle then?"

A real riot the three of them. Ha. Ha.

"Where I go to school we are taught never to generalize about people on the basis of nationality, " I shrieked. It was line right out of my text book.

"Little touchy aren't we?" Nana rolled her eyes and headed towards the door.

"Guess our little prima donna needs some quiet time." Mum kissed me on the nose .

"We'll be waiting in the car."

"Thank you all very much" I shouted out after them.

I turned back to the mirror. I adjusted my over-the-shoulder-boulder-holder so I wouldn't feel so lopsided. But there was another reason I need some last minute privacy.

I put my white heart-shaped rock on the dresser. It was supposed to be a wedding present. Anyhow. I added a note.

DEAR NANA,

I wanted you to have this. It isn't perfect. But I love it anyhow. You, too.

Minn.

Chin hair or no chin hair, vinegar smell and all.

The horn honked.

"TabisintacintheMirimichi!"

"Alright, already!"

—NOW—

Altostratus. Cumulonimbus . . .

Imagine if all these folks sitting down there in front of me knew the real story. They'd probably run for their lives or burn me at the stake or something. And anyhow, I'm still trying myself to figure out what *the truth the whole truth nothing but the truth* is. In that *cross your heart hope to die* kind of way.

"Now would you please join me in welcoming the young lady who is part of the reason we are here today, Cinnamon Elizabeth Hotchkiss."

That's my cue. I move to the podium as if I am walking on the bottom of the ocean floor. I do a Rigbyism-style pep talk. *You can do this! See yourself a winnah.* I do a creative visualization. I picture them all naked in front of me. It makes me giddy. I do a deep-breathing cleansing breath. Look up at the clouds. I touch the brim of my cap for comfort.

I can feel them. They are all here—crew and passengers, souls lost and soul saved from the SS *Atlantic.* Their loved ones. Stubby. My sister. Harv. And so many more. Here. *Now.*

I find my voice. The words are swimming on the page, but I rehearsed it backwards forwards upside down and in the tub. I know my speech by heart. Especially the last lines.

"In closing, ladies and gentlemen, I would like to quote part of a poem.

> *I am the daughter of the earth and water,*
> *And the nursling of the sky;*
> *I pass through the pores of the oceans and shores;*
> *I change, but I cannot die.*

"See, I think we are all sons and daughters of the earth and water, and maybe like Mr. Shelley wrote in this poem, we are like the clouds—we change, but we never really die. My grandmother says a spirit never dies as long as there is someone around to remember them. That is what we are doing. It's my Nana who made me see how important it was to save the grave. And John Hindley, a boy who lost his mother and father and his brother Ma— Thomas"—my voice trembles a bit here—"and his childhood in the same night and wanted us to remember them. May we never forget their loss and the bravery of those who helped in the rescue that night. Folks like the Clancys, like Reverend Ancient—ordinary folks who show us extraordinary things are possible. I would like to make special mention of Harv Jollymore—"

"A hero of a man!" The clapping is loud.

Nana is smiling up at me. Nodding. Brave as can be.

"And thanks to all of you, for it is the people of this community who are the real gravesavers."

Mr. Dubbins helps me unveil the portrait. "In the Mizzen," it's called. The clapping is louder. I gasp when I look at the painting. John is suspended in the rigging, but the mizzenmast, like a rope ladder, leads up from a cemetery. A girl who looks a lot like me is reaching up towards him. Mr. Dubbins painted John's eyes blue.

I have the job of throwing the dirt over the first of the bones. I place the baby's skull gently in the box.

I throw the dirt.

I do not cry.

The clouds are rolling back out to sea. The sun peeks through as Laura Smith starts singing. "My bonnie lies over the ocean . . ." Everyone is so still. And then there he is.

My Max. Thomas. Standing at the fringe of the crowd as real as anybody. He's dressed like always and wearing a hat. He bows low and salutes, fingers at the brim of his hat. I nod. John, behind him, waves. John disappears but Thomas lingers.

Cnicus benedictus! I don't want him to go. Maybe he'll be back, but I somehow doubt it.

I know what I have to do. To say.

I can't.

Thomas pleads with me. With those eyes.

"Farewell," I whisper finally. And just like that, with a smile of gratitude, he's gone, drifting together with the others in that cloud moving over the sea. It dissolves. Nothing but blue sky. So why do I have a sad throat? I swallow.

I turn back to my family and the rest of the crowd. They've joined in the singing.

Now, I know everyone says that I have a bit of an overactive imagination. And there's definitely some truth in that. But right now?

Above their voices, cross my heart, real as you or me or the wind, he whispers back.

Fare well. May you all fare well.

ACKNOWLEDGEMENTS

There are many to thank:

Kevin Sylvester, producer at CBC, commissioned the original short story where Minn was conceived. He was a most generous first editor. Shelagh Rogers narrated *Cinnamon Hotchkiss and the Flying Toboggan* in December 1997. In the cadence of her voice I heard Minn's first breath.

With the encouragement of Jane Buss, den mother, heart hugger and Executive Director of the Writer's Federation of Nova Scotia, I applied for a Nova Scotia Arts Council Explorations Grant in 1998. Without that timely financial assistance this book would not exist.

John Pearce, then at Doubleday Canada, suggested Minn belonged in a novel. For his support of my work and understanding of my idiosyncrasies over the years, I am deeply indebted. Suzanne Brandreth gave me faith and excellent questions to develop a sturdier version. Maya Mavjee, publisher of Doubleday Canada, had the vision to accept a book that doesn't fit easily into categories. I thank her for being a publisher who keeps open to otherness not only market. Amy Black, dream editor: your intelligence, intuition, and pen protected me from my worst faults. It was good to not be "alone" at sea any longer. Thank you for your skilled, sensitive hands on deck. Both manuscript and author are more ship-shape as a result. To all the Doubleday crew: your loyalty means everything. Lahring Tribe is incomparable.

Dr. Terry Punch, former neighbour, historian and geneal-ogist shared my initial entry into this world with enthusiasm and put expert research skills to work at the provincial archives. He produced a treasure trove of facts, and brought me the picture of John Hindley. To Pam Punch, your wise, intuitive and generous nature taught me lessons in courage and open-heartedness. Our kinship has given me much beyond words and faith in other worlds. Two other Chocolate Lake friends are linked to this book. Alex Astbury taught me to make a bowline knot and Faune Creaser connected me with Bill Matheson, who generously offered me a copy of *The Coal Was There For Burning* (Marine Media Management). Another book I found useful for background was Keith Hatchard's *The Two Atlantics* (Nimbus Publishing). Bruce Nunn passed on the name of Anne Bartlett who gave me a contact with a Hindley (Hanley) descendent. It was a fortu-itous meeting, which urged further exploration.

Jenny Durant and Melanie Colbert read, offered feedback, and helped fix typos in early stages.

To the McNally family—Danny and Freda and their daughters—for their help, especially to Danielle for lending me her training diary. And to Mary McNally, who supports authors by reading and buying their books I owe royal-ty thanks.

To my amazing women friends who listened all the while or gave cheerleading at crucial moments: Janet Blackwell, Karleen Bradford, Martha Brooks, Carol Bruneau, Gwen Davies, Maggie DesVries, Dawn Fisher-King, Thora Howell, Alison Gordan, Rachna Gilmore, Joan Tetzlaff, Pam Donoghue, Sara Filbee, Lian Goodall, Alma Lee, Janet Lunn, Mary Machiussi, Carol McDougall, Sue Newhook, Caroline Parry, Joanne Sadler, Shelley Tanaka, Marie Thompson, Dawna Ring, Noreen Smiley, Joanna Stanbridge, Nancy Watson, Deborah Wiles, Carol Campbell Williamson, and members of the Lethbridge and Ottawa Children's Literature Roundtables. Laura Smith allowed me to refer-ence her in name. Her version of "My Bonny Lies Over the Ocean" is on the CD Between *The Earth and My Soul*. Margot Brunelle, Rose Vaughan, Ian Wallace, and Barbara Mercer found their way into this book in disguise. . . .

To my community of friends at City Fitness in Washington, my refuge between pages—you lift the weight of the words off my shoulders.

My husband, Gilles, is anchor and life raft in the sea life I'm still dreaming. Your belief that even the roughest waters are navigatable gives me faith it might be so.

Finally, a special child named Julie Lalonde made me *promise* to tell people unicorns were real. There are no unicorns in this book. But during the writing of it, I saw one. I am so grateful for the precious time I had with Julie. Her spirit inspired all of us who knew her. She was the angel by my side during this long voyage of my imagination and often held my hand if not my pen.